FINDING CALEB

Book I of the Search and Rescue Dog Series

D1602604

SCOTT HAMMOND

Black Rose Writing | Texas

ISBN: 978-1-68513-195-1
PUBLISHED BY BLACK ROSE WRITING
www.blackrosewriting.com

Printed in the United States of America
Suggested Retail Price (SRP) $19.95

Finding Caleb is printed in Minion Pro

*As a planet-friendly publisher, Black Rose Writing does its best to eliminate unnecessary waste to reduce paper usage and energy costs, while never compromising the reading experience. As a result, the final word count vs. page count may not meet common expectations.

Edited by Barbara Hammond

ACKNOWLEDGEMENTS

To my wife, Barbara, who is the compass I carry in the wilderness of my life and the warm fire that welcomes me home.

To those who helped me find my fiction voice, including Caleb, Parker, Declan, Milo, Leo, Evelynn, Asher, Luke, Lea, Lindsey, and Raelynn. You are why I write.

And finally, thank you to all who search, rescue, and comfort people on the worst day of their lives.

FINDING CALEB

Superheroes do for us what we cannot do for ourselves. Marvel comics got it wrong. Real superheroes weigh under one hundred pounds, have a wet nose, big hearts, four paws, and often a bushy tail. They cannot fly or smash through things. They work quietly, invisibly in service of us, even though their life expectancy is just 12 to 14 years. Their superpower? A nose that smells 300-500 times better than any human, and a heart to serve until they can serve no more.

PART 1: LOST

CHAPTER 1

"Remember who you are!"

Mom shouted as I ran through the kitchen and out the door. My morning routine was down to a science. My alarm went off at 7:35 AM. Three minutes in the shower. By 7:40 AM I was dressed. Grabbed my already packed book bag off the desk. In one motion I ran through the kitchen family gauntlet, yelling a self-important "gotta go" to my mother who still tried to kiss me, and "bye dad" to my dad. Mom always gave a parenting cliché to the back of my head as I passed through the kitchen, grabbing toast or a pop tart on the way out the door. "Remember who you are," "Be your best self," or "You are here for a reason," were her favorites.

"Here" was a generic bedroom community in Massachusetts, twenty-six miles from Boston. "The reason" was because this is where my dad could get a job in a college town where education was the number one industry. I had quickly grown weary of telling my online gaming friends, "No, I'm not a Red Sox fan. No, I don't go to Patriots games. No, my dad does not work at Harvard." Harvard was the only university anyone not from Boston knew about in Boston.

Our little suburb town was once populated by hockey playing blue-collar New Englanders, but they could not stave off the invasion of English and Art professors from all over the U.S., okay, the world, who bought homes at 20% over market and pushed Massachusetts natives further away from Boston. This place was close enough to Boston to be convenient, far enough away to be affordable, and not prestigious enough to be attractive to the big buck techies or the business and engineering professors who live a little closer to Boston and in bigger, nicer houses.

But I digress. In my morning routine, it took exactly seven minutes to walk/run three blocks to school while eating breakfast. My freshly rested legs carried me past wood-framed houses built in the 1950s with the garages turned into family rooms or extra bedrooms. My path took me under the oak tree canopy to a tired old crossing guard at the corner. Then across the street and up the steps of the old stone block school building, through the doors, into the pulsing narrow halls, to my locker. One minute to open, get books, and paused to say "hi" to the cute girl two lockers away. Then ninety seconds to dance through the halls, now draining of students, and slip into class just as the bell rang.

On this day I arrived at Mr. White's current affairs class early, with 15 seconds to spare, and I dropped into my self-assigned seat on the back row of this class like a base runner stealing second. Mr. White did not assign seats, but there were clearly front row and back row sitters. I was a back-row sitter who enjoyed being invisible.

It bugged me that all the other students were already in place when I arrived. Everyone was in their seats, with notebooks opened, checking their daily schedules, and looking like responsible students who were hungry for knowledge. But my classmates were not hungry for knowledge. They were hungry for what they desired most- parental recognition. My parents usually recognized me with high praise when I woke up on time, did a chore, or ate my vegetables. The only way these kids could get parental recognition was with a report card with all As. My parents took an occasional, and yes, casual interest in my grades. But my peers lived in pressure cooker homes, sometimes with two college professor parents. Some parents taught at Harvard. For this lucky bunch, their value, access to transportation, emotional well-being, availability of video gaming, and even financial well-being, depended on getting good grades. After years of brainwashing by overachieving parents with misplaced ambitions, some even feared homelessness, or worse, a blue-collar job, if they got something less than an "A." The designated "cool guy" in the class, and every class has one, once said in a moment of complete honesty, "If I don't get into an Ivy League school for college, I won't be invited to family reunions for the rest of my life." Another girl said her parents, and both sets of grandparents, had been saving for her college education since before she was born. "They plan the size of our family based on how much tuition they think they will be able to afford."

My classmates were the children of parents who grew up as teacher's pets, and they were all expected to be teacher's pets. Mr. White had this figured out. He would talk about it openly, and he was clear. "Not everyone in this class will get an A," he would say at least once a week. He also would remind students, "I will never discuss your grade with your parents or guardians, only with you." He did that because parents would routinely pay a "courtesy visit" before official parent-teacher conferences to ever so subtly tell Mr. White that they expected their child to get an "A" in this "elective" class. These parents, who were fully credentialed scholars with a full rack of graduate degrees, considered teachers like Mr. White to be third-class thinkers in this world that ordered the importance of people by college degree, academic discipline, institutional prestige, and the number of published papers.

I was sure that my parents and Mr. White would never meet because my parents respected the people who instructed their children. They kept their distance and trusted well-trained educators to do their job well. They were also busy with their own problems. My father was still trying to make tenure. My mother was teaching adjunct and considering "an advanced degree" herself.

Mr. White caught my eye as I came sliding into class. "You ready, Caleb?" he asked. Quick memory scan. "Ready for what?" I thought. Oh. Panic. It was my day to open the class with a presentation. Suddenly I felt like I would rather be back in my bed dreaming that I had come to school without my pants on.

"Yes, sir."

The seasoned teacher recognized my lie, and subtly motioned to the stack of newspapers at the back of the room. He was old school and liked the dead tree way to deliver information. He kept day-old newspapers around a worn-out couch in the back of the class so that students like me, who had forgotten to do their assignment, could come to class early and do prep work. The Save the Whales Club wanted to call the fire marshal on him for having paper newspapers. They said paper is a fire hazard and he should go digital. But he still saved those newspapers that saved unprepared, sorry, back row students like me.

It was my day to start the class out with a three-minute presentation on how this "current event had an impact on my life." It was a lame way for a high school teacher to make current affairs relevant to a group of students who started studying for their ACTs just after preschool graduation. Most students began their presentations with a long "uh, well." Then they would look at their feet. Fiddle with their hands. Suddenly, they realized their hair was on fire. There was some kind of apology. "I'm sorry, I really didn't really prepare well, "or "I couldn't find..." and "I really didn't feel well." You could see Mr. White taking notes, preparing so he will have appropriate documentation for parents when they challenge the grade.

While I was at the back of the room preparing to not make any of those mistakes, Mr. White took his time making announcements. "The upcoming prom, blah blah. The game and the need to support the team, blah blah. Representatives from this elite college, blah blah." "The robotics club, blah blah."

I had 45 seconds to do 45 minutes of prep work. I picked up the first paper I could see. Ah, the Denver Post. A western newspaper written for a place people from Boston consider to be an occupied foreign country - the western United States. According to the culture of the East Coast intelligencia, no educated people lived in the west, except in communities surrounding islands of culture called Stanford and Caltech, and government laboratories. The west is a place to ski, to extract oil, and for summer road trips to national parks. It is not a place where serious people would be taken seriously.

But I had lived there, so maybe I could quickly find an article that affected me at a personal level. I could wow these kids who I wanted to know by showing them something about the wonderful west. Mr. White was finishing the announcements, so I stood up and started walking slowly and confidently towards the front of the room. "I got this." I spent precious nanoseconds giving myself a little pep talk. With a brief introduction, Mr. White reminded my classmates that I was "new" and from "out west," then sat down at his desk, turning the class over to me.

I had 180 seconds to get a wow. I took the local section of the Post, hoping for an opportunity to ad lib something brilliant. Then I looked directly at the class, smiled, and glanced at the paper again, not realizing I had burned seven seconds of airtime in silence. The designated "cool guy" who was sitting in the front row said, "Giddy up, cowboy." There were snickers. "Cowboy" was the class nickname for me that was hardly ever used because I was hardly ever seen. Never mind that I had never been on a horse or touched a cow.

But I did not let that snarky line put me off my game. I had found a dateline for Lincoln County. I figured I could give this a good spin because I had spent five summers of my life in Lincoln County. Wonderful summers. While all these eastern kids were shipped off to summer camps in Maine and Vermont, never more than a mile from a doctor and a MacDonald's, I had spent my summers near, and sometimes in, the real wilderness.

I faced down the class, then read aloud the headline, "Beloved Search Dog…" I choked. There was a lump in my throat. "Beloved search dog dies," My once reliable voice squeaked out. Then I put my hand over my eyes, turned my back on the class and cried like a little boy.

CHAPTER 2

A 16-year-old high school boy whose body, mind and soul exists in the space between boy and man, is not supposed to cry. At this age, in front of these people, you don't even admit that you cried when you were a baby. You especially don't tear up and sniffle in front of others. If you do, you will never get a date. Never get more than a "B." No one will ever talk to you. They will only talk about you. About how you cried in front of the class. Crying is worse than the scarlet letter we read about in English, or the botched tattoo that one of the senior football players got on his bicep. Or getting in a fender bender the first time your parents let you take the car out on your own on the day you get your driver's license, and a cute girl is sitting next to you.

In private, high school boys cry for two reasons, neither of them good. The first is because they are hurt. Like a sports injury or a breakup with a girlfriend. The second reason is that you are embarrassed because you are crying. Yes. You are so embarrassed that you are crying, and that it makes you cry. It's a vicious circle. You are crying because you don't want people to see you crying.

But I was not thinking about any of that. This was uncontrollable grief. My knees began to weaken. My voice broke and my eyes burned. Then my nose began flowing snot, and my eyes began flowing salty tears, and fluids converged where my mustache was going to be when I was old enough to grow something more than peach fuzz. All I could offer the class was strange convulsive breathing noises. From behind my wall of tears, everything was moving in slow motion.

Someone, I don't know who, placed a chair under me. I felt Mr. White's gentle hand on my shoulder, guiding me to the seat. Out of the corner of my eye, I saw Emily Smyth grab a box of tissues from the teacher's desk and put it on my lap. I quickly grabbed a handful and pressed them to my face. Blinded by the burning tears, I expected to hear the class begin snarky comments. Yes, after the mocking and humiliation, I would need to find another school. Things were over for me here. But as the moments passed, I heard nothing. Through the fog of the fluid still streaming from my eyes, and the overwhelming pain in my core, I saw genuine concern on the faces of my classmates. Even the back row had stood up and moved up to be closer, as the class formed an impromptu and therapeutic semicircle around me.

I fought to regain my composure, and at first, that just made it worse. The designated cool guy said, "It's OK, Cowboy." I blubbered a little, then blew my nose without restraint into the tissue. No one said, "gross." No one said "uncool." No one said anything. They just looked at me kindly while I felt like a semi-truck involved a multi-car wreck on the freeway.

After a minute, which felt like a day, I looked up and tried to make eye contact. I forced a smile and then rubbed my head and eyes. "That's Boo," I choked out a line while looking at my feet. "Who?" asked Emily. She was sitting closest to me and was the most experienced crier in the class. Whenever a class member did their presentation on homelessness, hunger, puppies, or little children, you could count on Emily unashamedly tearing up and sometimes dramatically and publicly shedding tears. The social rules for crying were different for girls.

I looked at Emily and said, "Boo who?" with a crooked smile. The class laughed an abbreviated but sincere laugh. Like the release of pressure in an old locomotive, the tension in the room vaporized like steam. My classmates focused on Mr. White. He was the jungle guide who would take the class through this unfamiliar terrain of collective honesty and raw emotion.

Mr. White gently took the newspaper out of my hands and held up the picture of a stout, blonde Golden Retriever standing at attention on a rock and wearing a vest that said, "Search and Rescue." He then took his reading glasses out of his pocket, balanced them carefully on his nose, pausing for dramatic effect, and read the newspaper article:

"Lincoln County, Wyoming- A search and rescue dog known as "Boo the-Wonder-Dog" died from injuries sustained while searching for a missing 3-year-old girl on Saturday. The girl was found safe with the injured dog by her side. Boo later died of his injuries. Lincoln County Search and Rescue Director, and Deputy Nate Garner, who was also Boo's handler said, "Boo has helped over twenty people return home."

Thirty volunteers helped bring the dog and the girl down from Daggett Lake in the High Uinta Wilderness Area near the border between Wyoming and Utah. Garner says Boo broke his back while tracking the missing girl. He said the elderly dog continued to search until he found the girl, then could no longer move. "Boo was getting up there in years," said Garner. He was 12 years old and suffering from arthritis, which is common in his breed. But he still loved to search, and he was very good at it."

A "Go Fund Me" page has been set up to help buy a dog to replace Boo on the Lincoln County Search and Rescue Team, but Deputy Garner says, "You can't replace a dog like Boo. Not now. Not ever."

My sobs came again for a moment. Emily and the other girls joined in. The semi-circle got closer as everyone in the class emotionally connected like the flickering lights on a Christmas tree. Mr. White's grip on my shoulder was more pronounced. The boys were uncomfortable, surprised by this unexpected emotional trip, but they still moved in on the semicircle, not wanting to miss the intimacy that was so rarely found in the high school experience. I took another tissue, then another, then offered the box to Emily, and she passed it around to the other criers. When the room had stilled to just sniffles, I cranked my head around to Mr. White. I felt like I owed him an explanation for my dramatic disruption of his class. I assume I had taken more than my three minutes by now, and he needed to know the reason.

I looked at Mr. White and saw his eyes inviting honesty. I said, "That's the dog that saved my life. Twice."

CHAPTER 3

Frances Leon White was a "cool" teacher, even though he did not let the students call him by his first name. The only name he hated more than his first name was his middle name. The only time he had ever sent a student to the office in 22 years of teaching was when a student, on a bet, called him by his middle name in front of the entire class. A one day in-school suspension and a ten-page apology letter later, and the word was out. Everyone knew you do not call Mr. White by his first or middle name, or your college diploma might have the words "trade tech" on it.

Mr. White was a social studies teacher who had taken the unwanted assignment to teach five sections of current affairs, not because he was no longer interested in Ancient, American, or World History. In fact, those were his favorite subjects. He loved to tell 15-year-olds about the "Age of Reason" and the birth of American Democracy. He had taught Madison and Adams like they were the Psalms or the Koran and ignited flames of interest in students that lasted a lifetime. After he had been married for ten years, his wife became ill. Teaching current affairs meant he could go home every day when school was out, without papers to grade. He would take over the nursing care of his wife, cook dinner, put the children to bed, then watch CNN, BBC, NBC, and Fox News with his wife until the pain meds took the conversation and the consciousness away.

The pain of her death and the difficulty of raising two children alone made him grateful for the easily compartmentalized teaching assignment of current affairs, even though he was often reminded by over ambitious parents that this subject was not an important enough to be on the SAT, ergo every "serious" student deserved an "A." Teaching current affairs, and having the "cool teacher" label, made Mr. White unpopular with his colleagues in the faculty lounge. He didn't care. He spent what little spare time he had in his classroom or talking with students. Even though he did not teach the subject of his passion, he taught with passion, and regularly ignited activism, exploration, and discovery in students. Around his room there were photos of his former students who had gone on to bigger and better things. Several were judges. One was a congressperson. There were CEOs and the leaders of NGOs. There was even a moderately famous soap opera actor. Sometimes these former students would just show up in the middle of a class. After a wink and a nod, Mr. White would introduce them like they were best friends, and they would tell a story, or pretend to lead a discussion while really showing us what it was going to be like for us in ten or fifteen years if we were successful. Students often joked about having a life worthy of making it onto Mr. White's informal hall of fame. Me? I just wanted to collect a passing grade and move on. I did not want to be memorable or even mentionable. I just wanted to pass the class with a "C" or better, pass the 10th grade, and pass on to life.

And yet here I was, suddenly the center of attention, with Mr. White looking right at me. He had been assigning students to make presentations on how a current event affected their life for years. Presentations that were usually the most forgettable three minutes of the school day, that often began with a student saying something like, "My stepdad's second cousin's ex-wife's father who I have never met is connected to this story because…" Never did a student take a story on opioid addiction and describe how his father's dependency on pain medications had ruined their family. Those kinds of honest discussions happened in the halls and locker rooms, but not in class. Mr. White had sat through hundreds of boring, just good enough presentations for this golden moment. He looked at me, and not the class, and said in a quiet voice that everyone could hear," Thank you Caleb, now how did this dog save your life?"

And so, I began the story that had changed my life, and that would change it again.

"When I was nine, we lived in Iowa, you know, in the Midwest. They've got farms, wheat and corn, barns and abandoned trucks, and flat fields everywhere. Kids in Iowa grow up driving tractors when they are eight and play with water snakes. They also have a good university where my dad was going to graduate school."

I could see I had made a connection. The kids in this class had less than fond memories of when one or more parents were in graduate school.

We lived in an old farmhouse that leaked air. Hot air in the winter and chilly air in the summer. My mom said the walls did not break the Iowa wind, they just slowed it down. The old farmer who owned the place had raised a long-gone family in the house, and he was loose on collecting rent. Sometimes we would work for rent on the little patch he still farmed. He knew my dad was finishing his PhD in English and my mom was trying to keep food on the table. Between his farm and our garden, and cash contributions from grandparents, we had food, but no table. It had been turned into my dad's desk, so we ate on the front porch or around the coffee table in the living room.

The summer I was nine was the worst. I remember mom and dad fighting, so there were slamming doors and yelling, and my dad occasionally sleeping on the couch. To make it worse, I was wearing "hand me downs" even though I did not have a big brother who would hand down used clothing. It came from a charity closet at the church the old farmer attended. Our big family fun was piling in the minivan with bald tires and getting a 50-cent ice cream cone at the Dairy Queen from the real dairy queen who rode on a float in the Fourth of July parade. After meeting her, I assumed that the British Royalty my mom read about in the newspaper also worked at a corner drive-in somewhere near Oxford, serving malts, hamburgers, and cheap ice cream while wearing a short skirt and roller skates.

"One afternoon during summer vacation, my parents had a big fight about my dad changing his dissertation topic or something. I got tired of it all. I mean. I was just a kid, and when they would fight, I would disappear into my room or out in the cornfields while they had words. They could not see me, and I assumed they did not care. One time I ran away. I took my Game Boy, a radio, a pack of crackers and my favorite blanket and went over to the old barn behind the farmer's house. I decided I would rather live in his hay loft alone than with two warring adults.

I thought they would not notice my absence, but boy, was I wrong. The farmer saw me moving into the barn, and within minutes, Mom and Dad were standing above me in the hay, inviting me to come home. When I declined their invitation, more influence was provided until finally I was carried home. The house not only leaked air, it leaked sound. That night and all the next day there were whispers and closed doors, and phone calls in hushed voices. I heard the word "stress" in every sentence. I picked up other words like "Lincoln, Marge, play with Billy," and, "I'm sure it will be fine." I wondered if running away had caused my parents to get a divorce. One night, my mom casually announced over dinner that she and dad were going to get "counseling" while I was going to live with Aunt Marge in Wyoming while "mom and dad work things out." Marge had an eleven-year-old boy named "Billy," and he would be a good "big brother" for me.

To my parents I said, "OK, no problem." But I was scared. To me, Wyoming was the name of a prison. "Aunt Marge" was the name of the sadistic warden who would feed me bread and water. And "Billy" was going to be my cellmate and nemesis, who would turn on me in the prison yard if I didn't give him my care packages. Seeing my face, Mom reminded me it would just be for a few weeks, which for me might as well have been 20 years-to-life. Still, I was happy that the word "divorce" was not included in this announcement and that I was not being blamed. So, not wanting to add conflict in the family, I kept my mouth shut and resigned myself to my sentence.

The night before we left, I could hear my mom and dad talking, and my mother's soft crying, until the early hours of the morning. I finally fell asleep just as the eastern sky was turning gray, and within an hour, my father carried my limp body to the back seat of the van. I awoke to see my mother and father kissing. Mom stepped back for a moment, then opened the driver's door. She turned and gave my father another kiss, this time in full view of her son. I remember thinking that was a good sign. I heard mom start the engine and felt the gentle rocking of the aged minivan and heard the crackle of tires on the popcorn gravel as sleep drew me back to obscurity.

Later, I awoke and was offered a peanut butter and jelly sandwich for lunch. Mom was not a fast driver, and so as we rambled down I-80 towards the Rocky Mountains, the big rigs were always passing us. I could see Dominion Freight, England Trucking, Allied Van Lines, even an elderly couple in a giant Winnebago came floating by as I lay on my back in the middle seat with the seat belt only symbolically buckled around my legs. When the batteries on my Game Boy died, I rolled down the window and tried to get the trucks to honk their horns by pumping my arm. When my dad was around, this was usually not allowed. But my mom's guilt gave me more freedom. Finally, a truck with a special custom set of pipes let out a noise like a submarine getting ready to dive. Mom laughed and gave me an "air" high five. It was good to see her with a genuine smile.

I dozed again, and I must have been out for a long time, because I had no recollection of how far we traveled or even what direction we went. I only remember arriving in this small town framed in a blue sky with mountains in the background. Mom said, "You're going to like it here…Lincoln River, Wyoming, where I grew up." The voice inside me was raging. Like it? How could I like it? I didn't know anyone. I didn't know where I was, and the people who were going to care for me did not know me. I would rather be dropped at a truck stop. Besides, if this place where you grew up was so magical, then why don't you and dad and I live here now?"As we drove down main street, I wondered if once my mom left Aunt Marge would issue me an orange prison jumpsuit and put me on the work gang.

Main Street in Lincoln River, Wyoming, was mostly empty. We passed the police station, a church, and boarded-up buildings, then turned left up a hill, past houses, then right onto an all-American street with white board houses, red brick houses, and green lawns. Mom stopped at mid-block in front of a sagging white board house with a large porch that looked like it was about to fall off the front of the house. She got out and slid the middle door of the van open, urging me to get all my stuff. There were kids of various ages playing an organized game on the street. In Iowa, kids lived miles apart on farms and had lists of chores they did before school and after school, so we never had neighborhood kid games. As I stepped out of the van, the kids in the game stopped, went silent, and turned their attention to me, like I had just stepped out of a spaceship onto planet Wyoming. The silence attracted moms who wondered if something was wrong and looked out the windows or stepped onto the porches. As I went from curb to house with my head down, a backpack on my back, and a bag in each hand, I felt like a prisoner doing the perp walk on the six o'clock news.

But this scene of self-pity was cut short as Aunt Marge burst out of the front door, nearly knocking the door off its hinges. She launched herself off the front porch, proving finally that fat people can fly, and came barreling down the front lawn, still carrying a dish towel and jiggling on every part of her body. Aunt Marge was an awful cook, a worse driver, and a world class hugger. Rumor had it that she had retired from the women's professional wrestling circuit and that her hugs had helped her earn one of those oversized trophy belts. As outrageous as it sounded, I believed it. She did not give the polite hugs that you get when you meet a relative or close friend. She gave the kinds of hugs that pulled you into her suffocating rolls of flesh and gave you a scent of the soap she used in the bathtub that morning. Her killer hugs were followed by unrestrained kisses on the forehead and fingers in your hair. I never waited long enough to see what was next, but she was strong enough that she could kill you with a body slam if you did not submit.

In the middle of the front yard, Marge positioned mom in front of her, and for a moment I thought Marge was going to pick her up and throw her onto the turf. Instead, she embraced her like she was an air mattress she was trying to deflate. It took every ounce of will mom had to keep molecules of oxygen headed towards her lungs. Marge knew just when her victims were about to pass out, and she let go and turned to me. I quickly extended my hand, trying to divert her with a handshake. But she was undeterred. "We'll have none of that," she muttered. Then she grabbed me, spun me around and embraced me in one move. Her squeeze-the-juice-out-of-me hug came with wet kisses on my forehead as she lifted me off my feet and swung me back and forth until I was dizzy and sick to my stomach.

She quickly herded us up to the front porch where the prying neighbors had to stretch their necks to have a full view. They did not want to miss this scene. Holding us at arm's length, she began by asking and answering her own questions. "I'll bet you are tired. Oh, Sure you are. You have been driving all day." "You must be famished?" she asked. Then answering her own question while we both tried to recover from oxygen deprivation, "Sure you are." After a one-person question-answer session, Marge ushered us into the house that smelled lived in and looked like it was cleaned every couple of months, whether it needed it or not. We were herded through the living room and to the kitchen table, then plopped down in the only two matching chairs of the set of six. Marge continued to do the talking while working in a whirlwind. In five minutes, she had whipped up a five-course meal with dessert while talking to my mom about people I did not know, or care to know. For Marge, the success of a meal was measured in volume, and the microwave oven was her friend. She moved carrots, potatoes, rolls, green Jell-O, and something she called meatloaf from the freezer into the microwave onto my plate. Without asking, she ladled thick brown, slightly burnt gravy over it all. She called it "grub," and it tasted like it. But at least I would not starve to death.

Halfway through the meal, my cousin Billy, who had been promised to me as a friend, came into the kitchen, attracted by the smell of meatloaf and slightly burnt gravy. "Billy," Marge said, switching from a sugary voice for visitors to a sandpaper harsh voice for her son, "This is your cousin Caleb. He's going to be sharing your room. Now show him his bed and help him get his things out of the hall!" There was no "please," and she stopped just short of saying "or else." Aunt Marge and Billy clearly had an adversarial relationship that was currently in a truce phase with no open hostilities, but he wasn't about to help me with my stuff without a threat from his mother.

Billy was the youngest in a family of nine kids. One of two still at home. The others were married or going to college in Florida or Alaska, or the Marshall Islands. Anyplace that was far from Lincoln, Wyoming. There was a semi-visible daughter who was in her last year of high school. Her name was Shellie, but Marge and Billy never talked about her. She was only seen occasionally in comings and goings from her locked room at the end of the hall. When she was seen, she looked like she had been peeled off the cover of Elle magazine and dropped onto planet Wyoming to be raised by alien creatures. Shellie was smart, beautiful, articulate, clean, organized, everything the rest of the family was not.

Billy reluctantly took me to the hall and pointed at Shellie's room. "Never go in there," he said, not inviting a "why" question. In his room, he showed me a cot in the corner where I would sleep. "Keep your junk under your bed," he said. Then he announced, "I'm eleven, almost eleven-and-a-half, so I don't play stupid kids' games." He paused to make sure I understood. Then, without another word, he disappeared out the window, into the yard, and then over the fence.

I wandered back into the kitchen, where Mom and Marge were fully engaged in family gossip. Stories about health conditions, pregnancies, and brushes with the law. Nothing that interested me. I just wanted to be home in my house with my parents in my life in Iowa. So, I went into Billy's bedroom, planted myself face down on my cot and thought about an escape.

Within minutes, Aunt Marge and Mom came into my room and I could see Mom was tearing up. In her quiet voice, she began telling me I was a "big boy," and it was only for a "little while" and that I could not be in a "better place." Then she helped me roll out my sleeping bag, gave me my favorite pillow from home, and kissed me "good night." Even though it was still light outside, I could see her out the window heading down to the van before she lost control of her emotions. She would drive for three or four hours, then sleep in the back of the van and finish the trip in the morning. I lay awake for an hour, listening to Marge shut down the house for the night. She cleaned the kitchen, made phone calls, and then called from the front porch for Billy. I'm not sure, but I thought I could hear her voice echoing off the mountains. I am sure that the whole town, unless they were stone deaf, could hear her sandpaper voice. It took 15 minutes of the Aunt Marge public PA pleading to bring the little rebel home, and by then I was drifting off to sleep with a still full stomach of that thing called meatloaf gurgling in my mid parts.

I awoke mid-morning with the sun spilling directly into the room to the sound of Billy killing monsters on his computer's video screen. He was in a trance, unwilling to be bothered, so I stumbled into the kitchen, found milk in the fridge and breakfast cereal on the table, and with a bowl in the cupboard, made my own breakfast.

To my surprise, Shellie walked in the back door wearing workout clothes. "Hi Caleb," she said, like we had known each other for years. She smiled an electric smile, pausing just long enough for us to make eye contact, then went to her room. "Wow. She is like a movie star," I thought, as my mouth opened wide and stayed that way until Marge appeared.

You could not accuse Marge of hiding her moods. No. Yesterday's bubbly welcome had been replaced with a case of the grumps. Her hair was rolled up in tiny tubes she called "curlers," and she was wearing an enormous cloth sack designed to leave everything to the imagination she called a "muumuu." I'm sure she could read the shock on my face, so before could say anything she announced that "most of the family," she pointed her nose at Shellie's room at the end of the hall, was going to a church picnic after lunch, and so I needed to wash and get ready now by having a shower and putting on my play clothes. I had never been to a church picnic. I did not know what to do to get ready, so took a quick shower, changed into my clean shorts, and packed my backpack with extras "just in case." Then I sat on my cot for three hours while "most of the family" got ready.

"Most of the family" for Marge was Billy and me. Her nameless husband and the father of her hoard of children seemed to have to work all the time at the local Walmart where he was an assistant manager. He was in a perpetual state of exhaustion and sent off a "don't talk to me, please" kind of vibe. He was occasionally seen mowing the lawn or on his way to the bathroom in the middle of the night.

After coaxing and threats, Billy and I were strapped in the back seat of an old station wagon with a crooked license plate and faded paint. The car surged down the patches of broken concrete they called a driveway, just as a late model recently buffed Black Lexus pulled in front of the house. "Shellie's boyfriend," Billy said with disgust. Behind the dark tinted windshield, I could see the silhouette of a perfectly shaped cowboy hat. As the black leather clad boyfriend want-to-be emerged from the car, Aunt Marge tapped the gas just enough to spin the wheels and create a cloud of dust from the broken gutter that ruined the picture of all black perfection the suitor was trying to project. Without acknowledging her faux pas, and with a great deal of self-satisfaction, Marge headed down the middle of the road with the radio blasting Garth Brooks and Taylor Swift. Nine or ten turns later, we twisted up a gravel road and arrived at a grassy hilltop where about a hundred happy people were cooking, talking, playing, and eating. Aunt Marge grabbed the plate of potluck cookies that had been gathering dust on the seat between Billy and me and stepped out of the car. She forgot us for a moment as the magnetic pull of her small-town peers drew her like a zombie towards a group of women. But then she turned around and said in her harsh voice, "Billy, you make sure that boy (pointing at me) has someone to play with."

CHAPTER 4

Billy did not do homework, make his bed, clean his room, or take care of his younger cousin without more than a barked order from his mother. He needed a threat with a detailed high impact punishment before he could take any action demanded by an adult. He waited for Aunt Marge to refocus on her waiting gossip partners, then he looked at me and said sarcastically, "See you later."

I was relieved that I would not be Billy's show-and-tell project with his friends, who were likely to be equally obnoxious. As he headed off to join his Wyoming home boys, I thought about how I would get to my home in Iowa. So, I stepped out of the hot car and into the dusty parking lot. Billy had his Magic cards out and had already staked out the only available shade trees in this park to play cards with his friends. If they couldn't play video games, Magic cards would have to do. There was a softball game and frisbee football on the mostly dirt playing fields, and a couple of dogs running around stealing food from picnic tables while being chased by their owners. Aunt Marge was 150 feet away, fully engaged with a half-dozen women who were all black belts in town gossip. I was sure that my story was being told as a tragedy because Marge was doing the talking, and women were dropping their jaws, clicking their tongues, and shaking their heads. I suspected my mom and dad were the antagonists. Marge was the hero of her own story, and I was the poor little boy who needed her help.

My best escape route was past a group of teenagers who were down by the stream, standing in groups and talking. As I stood there by the dusty minivan, a woman carrying a baby and a grocery bag in one arm and pulling a toddler by the hand with the other shuffled by me. She was talking with the toddler about bathroom business, saying, "you're a big boy and you can wait to go potty." When she saw me, and I assume she detected family resemblance that I could not see. "You one of Marge's kids?" she asked.

Before I could say anything to confirm or deny my relationship, she handed me the grocery bag and said, "Take this to the dessert table," addressing me like she was giving marching orders to one of her much younger children. Then she paused and said, "Oh. Please and thank-you," with her back already to me as she urgently dragged her kid towards the green row of portable out houses at the other end of the parking lot. At first, I was reluctant to look in the bag, but then I realized that even though there were people all around, no one was paying any attention to me. I opened the bag and inside I found a cheap plastic disposable tablecloth, a packet of handy wipes which I assumed would be missed as soon as she cleaned up the toddler, an unopened large package of Oreo cookies, and a small toy police car with an electric red light on top that really glowed. The siren on the car had been disconnected, to preserve the mental health of the mother. That, too, would be missed by the toddler while he was enduring the humiliation of his mother removing his messy pants.

I now know how Moses felt when the Red Sea parted, because in that moment I could see my way home. "Wow," my nine-year-old mind thought. This is just what I need to get back to Iowa. A perfect stash of supplies for my escape, thinking mostly of the cookies. I was dressed in shorts, a tee shirt, and tennis shoes with no socks. I had a backpack with a jacket and a water bottle. How could I pass up such a fantastic opportunity? If I started now, I might get there just after dark.

I set off in the hot afternoon sun, walking with purpose so as not to attract attention. I walked past various groups of adult strangers who had gathered by gender, who paid no attention to me. While preparing food, the women were ritualistically spilling out the news of this small town, prefaced with praises like "You are not supposed to know, but…" and "She would kill me if she heard me say this but…" The men were talking about trucks, crops, and cows, while lighting charcoal or preparing meat. Teenage girls were talking about the cute boys while passing looks to a group of teenage boys who were talking about the cute girls and simultaneously pretending the nearby girls did not exist. But I was an invisible stranger, and I thought I could see Iowa just over the horizon. So, I headed out in the opposite direction from which we drove into the picnic grounds. I found an opening in the fence and followed a well-worn trail towards a stream that for one month every year qualified as a river. A group of teenage boys and girls were sitting on large rocks near the river talking to each other. One boy, who was doing the talking, would turn around and throw a rock in the river occasionally. He was the one who saw me.

"Hey kid! Stay away from the water. You're not supposed to be down here." He barked in a voice designed to impress the girls more than scare me. I supposed these young adults were assigned to make sure the kids did not go down to the water. But they were not taking their assignment seriously. After yelling at me, this stream guard turned away and focused his attention on a giggling girl and his other adoring fans. I paused, as if I was going to comply, then continued to the banks of the river. Seeing this was just the right place to cross, I walked across a little patch of sand and launched myself onto a boulder. Then I hopped from boulder to boulder to the other side without getting wet. I scrambled up the other side, then crouched down in the grass and looked at the team of teenage river guardians. The young man looked over at the river, then at the trail that led back to the picnic grounds, then went on with his conversation. He had not seen me floating face down in the water, so he went back to focusing his attention on the young woman.

I was free. I would be in my bed in Iowa before Aunt Marge, Billy, and these Wyoming hillbillies even knew I was gone. There was another fence on the other side of the river, which I rolled under. On the grassy side of the fence, I followed an on again, off again trail for about a mile to a dirt road. "Not every road to Iowa was a freeway," I told myself. I knew I needed to get over the distant hills to get to home, and the road headed straight to the hills and away from the town, the picnic grounds, Billy, and Aunt Marge.

The road was just wide enough for an ATV or a four-wheel-drive jeep, but I thought it was a well-used trail where I might run into someone. I needed to be ready with a story. If I saw anyone, I would tell them I was on my way to school. If you told grown-ups you were going to school, they always let you pass because they did not want to cause you to be late. It did not occur to me it was Saturday afternoon in the summer. But it didn't matter. This was Wyoming, and I didn't run into anyone on the trail.

I followed the two tracks for a while, an hour. I had converted my frustration to energy, so I was moving fast. It felt good to no longer be a temporary orphan stuck in a back-water Wyoming town with a family that put the "dis" in dysfunctional. The trail started up into the hills. Going up did not slow me down at first, but soon I sucked for air. Lincoln, Wyoming, is a higher elevation than Iowa, so oxygen is harder to come by. I slowed but did not stop. And I certainly did not turn around for fear that one of those stream guard teenagers had woken up to their duty and was following me.

I kept my eyes focused in front of me, watching the hills get closer with every step. I had to admit, they looked bigger when I got close. In fact, they were mountains. I had heard there were mountains in Wyoming. These might be the mountains I had heard about. Because I had grown up in Iowa, I did not have experience with mountains. I paused, and for a moment I had to chase the second thoughts out of my nine-year-old brain. This was not a promising idea. I turned around and could see out into a big valley. My eyes followed the road, which was now a trail, down the slope and across the grassy fields to the river that was now far away. I must be closer to home than the picnic, I thought. I shaded my eyes from the sun as I scanned where I had come from. The sun was hanging in the line of thin clouds a third of the way up from the horizon. In the distance, I could see a wisp of smoke coming up from the picnic ground hill. It was so far away that I could only see cars, but not people. I imagined they were roasting their hotdogs and marshmallows over the fire now, and talking about the kid from where? "Iowa. Yes. Iowa. He went home."

CHAPTER 5

Just weeks before, Iowa had been a lonely, dirty, hot, frustrating place where my fighting parents kept me isolated from other kids. But now, in my mind, it was a paradise. The distractions of a known place had vanished. All the warts had fallen off, and I could not wait to be back in my home state and hometown, and home. So, I faced the mountains in front of me, assuming Iowa was just on the other side.

The grocery bag with my stash was in my pack, and my churning stomach told me it would be time for dinner soon. I looked over my shoulder, back towards the hoard of churchgoers at the picnic. Instead of potato salad and blackened hot dogs in soggy smashed buns and burnt marshmallows for dessert, I would eat Oreos for dinner. I was the lucky one. Then in the distance, drifting on the light wind, I heard an engine, like a motorcycle. There were signs of motorized power sports everywhere in these mountains. ATVs, ORVs, motorcycles. Every farm in Iowa had one of these off-road rockets that took farmers from house to field. I had also seen these mechanical chariots at the picnic being used to ferry food from the parking lot to the table. I looked behind me, paused, and listened. Then the sound faded.

The engine sound brought me to consider a scary possibility. What if the Oreos are missed? The church goers might hold an inquisition, and it might be determined that I had stolen the Oreos, or at least taken more than my share. I imagined an angry mob of Oreo deprived church goers willing to do whatever it took to retrieve their expected desert.

The teenagers who guarded the river would be dispatched at this very minute to find me and to recapture the Oreos. If they caught me, Aunt Marge would put me in time out on the cot in Billy's room.

If they were looking for me, the Oreo thief, I needed to hustle. So, I settled into a faster pace, scrambling off the trail that now switched back up the slope. The evening sun was still hot, and my throat was burning with thirst. It had been at least an hour since I had drained my water bottle. The trail leveled out again, and I crossed the green field and watched the trail dissolved in the meadow. But I confidently followed the direction of the trail on the other side of the level meadow. I bushwhacked through scrub oak and small pine trees to another ridge, and then over the ridge, not realizing that I was headed into a designated wilderness area.

As I had gained altitude, the terrain shifted from high green grasses and scrub oak to tall aspen trees and evergreens. "I was in Iowa yet?" I wondered. This was still Wyoming or Colorado. Yes. I needed to go through Colorado to get to Iowa. My first-grade geography class was kicking in. The mountains would be in Colorado, and once I crossed the mountains, in an hour, I would head down to my house in Iowa. I was convinced that my distorted map of the world was accurate, and that the well-meaning abandonment of me by my parents justified my escape from Marge, Billy and the potato salad people at the picnic in Lincoln, Wyoming.

As I bushwhacked my way up the next ridge, my throat felt like tree bark. My lips were dry, and my tongue was swelling. But I kept going, saying I would eat and drink once I was over the ridge and could see home. But at the top of the ridge the only thing I could see was another ridge and the mountain peaks with snow still on them looming in front of me. Colorado (it was still Wyoming) was bigger than I had thought. Each ride was steeper. On the other side of the next ridge was a steep rockslide into a canyon. The floor of the canyon was obscured by blue-toned evergreens. Something deep inside, even primal, told me I would find water in the trees. I paused and listened, and I could hear a breeze rustling the tree leaves, and I thought I could hear water over rocks. It was wishful thinking, but it added hope to my next steps, and made me feel all the thirstier.

The way down the rock field into the canyon was like nothing I had ever done in Iowa. The loose rocks crumbled under my feet and started rolling, gaining momentum, and tumbling into the trees below. I slipped a few times and even rolled once. But I stopped my momentum before I became like a rock tumbling out of control. I was scared, but I did not cry, even though I had collected cuts and bruises with every miscalculation.

The steep path gave way to level ground, with dense underbrush that tore at my exposed legs and scratched my arms, but in the jungle-like bushes I could clearly hear the hopeful sound that would relieve my thirst. Running water. I pushed myself through willows and tall grass, and before I saw the water, I stepped in it. My canvas tennis sneakers offered no protection, and the brackish chocolate milk water brought comfort to my feet and quickly cooled my overheated toes. But the relief soon turned on me and my feet became cold. Only hours earlier that water had been snow, and as it melted it had mixed with mud and muck. It did not look like something I wanted to drink, but I did anyway. I can't say whether the water was good or bad. It tasted unusual and was gritty. But it quenched my thirst and settled my hungry stomach. I took the water bottle out of the pack and filled it. It might be my only chance.

Fallen trees were everywhere in this narrow marsh. I sat on one with my feet out of the chilly water. I could see the shadows of the trees getting longer, but I could not stay here. So, I crossed over the little canyon and went up the other side that was as steep as what I had just come down. I found that going up was easier than coming down. By the time I had climbed out of the canyon, the sun was going down. Just below me was a meadow, and at the edge of the meadow, even though I could not find a trail, there was a place where I could see that people had camped. There was a fire ring with partly burned garbage. About fifty feet away from the flat space where the tents pitched, silhouetted in the shadow's large rectangular shapes. As I approached, I could see hay bales. I was from Iowa, and I knew what hay bales looked like. This was a piece of home. Something familiar. So, I sat down on the straw, opened my Oreos, and ate.

The Oreo tasted better than any Oreo I had ever tasted. It was sweet and chocolaty, and I imagined my teeth were stained black with the crumbs. I took another, then another. I opened the water bottle, and forgetting where it came from, I sloshed it into my throat. The silty brown water seemed no different from the spring water we drank in Iowa. It was refreshing. I had more cookies. More water. All the time, it was getting darker. But I was too involved in my famished self-indulgence to worry. I leaned back and rolled off the bale of hay and into a pile of loose hay. It wasn't a big pile, but it was big enough to give a boy a good warm bed.

I do not remember what happened next. I was exhausted. Sleep pounced on me like a hungry mountain lion. My eyes closed, and I was gone.

Hunger woke me in the middle of the night. Buried in the hay, with my back to a bale, I was so warm and comfortable that for a moment I thought I was in my bed at home with my parents just down the hall. Then I rolled over on my backpack and felt something hard. I fumbled into the pack with my fingers, and light came on and I saw a red glow of the toy police car with the push button light on top, and I could see I was sleeping in the forest by myself in a big pile of hay. But I was too hungry to be afraid, and too thirsty to do anything but drink. I used the little glowing light to find the water bottle and drained what was left. Then I ate another cookie and as I did, I fell asleep thinking my mom would be proud that I slept all by myself in the hay under a tree when I walked home from Wyoming to Iowa.

· · ·

The bell rang, signaling the end of the class period. My three-minute presentation had taken the entire class period, and no one had stopped me, hurried me, or even asked a question. The forgiving audience had turned the serious social faux pas of my crying fit into a plus. Mr. White stood at the back of the class with a big smile on his face, like the baseball coach when one player hit a home run. The students all sat frozen in their seats, waiting for what would happen next. I looked up at the class, now self-conscious that I had taken the entire class period, only to see nods of appreciation.

Mr. White started slowly pacing at the back of the room. He had deliberately disconnected while I was speaking, and not interrupted, because as an expert teacher he recognized that sometimes the best learning comes when the keeper of the class gives up the space to a once quiet voice. Mr. White recognized that the telling of my story had ignited interest in the class, and it was an overwhelming success for the "how I was affected by this current event" assignment. But I think he could also see that it was helping me deal with my grief. It was helping me make sense of a tough time. It was helping me move from outsider to insider in a community that divided the world by ACT scores.

There was a burst of appeals from my fellow students all at once. "Mr. White, can we please…?" "Mr. White, it would be good if…" "Mr. White, how about…?" Mr. White raised his hand to signal silence. "We'll pick this up again tomorrow." The class sighed approval. He looked at me and waited. I gave him a nod, then headed out of class and into crowded halls and the daily classroom routine. It felt like a different school. The same place. The same people. But a different school.

CHAPTER 6

The toxic anxieties that haunted me and hindered sleep did not come that night. I drifted off to sleep thinking about my foolish run away when I was nine, my other life in Wyoming, and Boo. His kind eyes, cold nose, and warm soft fur. I was surprised at my confidence. I didn't worry about the next day in Mr. White's class. "Just let the story flow," I told myself. I needed to speak it as I had lived it, and I would be fine. I wasn't worried about the designated cool guy, or Emily Smyth, or how anyone would react. Just 24 hours ago these classmates were strangers to be feared. But their kindness and interest in hearing my story had changed that. They were not friends yet, but there was an opening that was an enormous opportunity.

I awoke at 7 AM without help from my alarm clock, showered, and dressed slowly. Just as I was ready to head downstairs, my alarm clock went off, reminding me that today was going to be different from yesterday. I opened the top drawer of my nightstand and took out the tokens, my treasures, that I would show my classmates today. Then, I walked calmly into the kitchen drawn by the smell of pancakes, bacon, and my dad's coffee. My mother was in her usual position at the stove, stirring blindly and trying to watch the morning news show, who was doing a story on "breakfast, the most important meal of the day." Dad was hovering over the coffeemaker, hoping that his stare would speed up its production cycle. Mom tried not to display shock when I sat down at the table, but her face betrayed her. She cleared her throat and asked in a sing-song syrupy voice, "Want breakfast?" She looked at Dad, and he gave a nod that I was not supposed to see. Then she heaped food intended for him in teenage sized portions onto my plate. He would do with just coffee today, that is if the coffee maker delivered on its promise.

Telling my story of deprivation, survival, and hunger in the Wyoming wilderness to my class yesterday made me hungry this morning. I wolfed down what mother had placed in front of me, chasing each bite with orange juice and, between bites, chatting with my parents as they pretended this was a normal daily occurrence. My mother might have but did not interrupt me to say, "Who are you? And what have you done with our son?" But before our conversation could take a radical turn like that, I patted my jaw dropping dad on the back, kissed my mom on the cheek, said, "Have a nice day," and launched out the door and headed to school. Both parents sat paralyzed with surprise as my father's half portion of coffee cooled in front of him, and my sister's pancakes burned on the stove. I am sure that once I was out of earshot, my parents wondered aloud if I had suffered a head injury in gym class, fallen in love, or was on drugs.

I walked down the sidewalk at an even pace, just seconds behind my usual time. While walking, I focused on my presentation. The class was mine today. I was expected to continue my story. Yesterday went well. I wanted to make today even better.

At school, as I walked through the halls, I was no longer invisible. People looked at me. Some even said, "Hi" like it was normal for me to be there. I walked into the class with one minute to bell time, past the back row, and up to the front of the room. Mr. White saw me enter and gave me an affirming nod. Emily Smyth had arrived before me, with the help of others, and the permission of Mr. White, set the chairs up in a semicircle with my chair facing everyone. The front row was already occupied, with Emily reserving the middle seat for herself with her backpack and a box of tissues, just in case. There were extra chairs from a neighboring class that were placed against the wall. Mr. White said there might be visitors. In under a minute, the room filled, and the focus was on me. The kid from the back row was in front of the class. Emily took her seat, looked at the class proudly, smiled at me, and said, "We're ready for you, Cowboy."

"I think I'm liking the nickname "Cowboy," I thought to myself.

Then I began again.

"The first thing that wakes you up in the morning are the birds. In the daylight, you don't really think much about birds. They occasionally fly into view, or call out a warning, but they are in the forest's background. But the birds own the early morning when they are on center stage and singing loud. It starts just as dark is dying and the sun is hinting at another day. They sing, and they are everywhere.

As I awoke after the first night of my runaway, I felt a primitive joy hearing the score of the earth's first symphony composed by God and performed by birds. I dozed in a half sleep until light spilled into my little hay fortress. During the night, and quite by instinct, I had pulled the hay over my legs, my torso, and even my head. With hay under me and hay over me, I was warm, comfortable, but still hungry and thirsty.

As I stirred, the chilly morning air seeped through my hay blanket and stunned my back. To recover my warmth, I needed to move, heading towards Iowa again. I waited until the sun heated the air, and I crawled out of my straw palace that I now know was left by an elk hunter who was bringing feed for his horses into the wilderness. He had never considered that leaving his bundle of hay behind because he got his elk on the first day of the hunt would save a nine-year-old from Iowa from hypothermia.

Before taking my direction, I walked around the elk camp. There was no garbage or beer cans. The horse dung had been scattered, and I could see that nothing useful had been left behind. There were nails in the trees to hang things on, and logs near the fire for the next camper to burn. I could see where the tents had been, and I could see a broken clothesline tied around a tree. I imagined they would return to this place every hunting season.

I did not know it, but I was becoming more observant. I was sensing more and connecting my feelings with what I was seeing. I tuned into my environment. As I scanned the camp, something seemed out of place. I looked again and had the same feeling, then I walked instinctively towards a large tree. Through the shadows, in the change of light and angles, I saw it. A treasure. In the dirt near a tree, with just the tip of a blade sticking out, was a pocketknife. The elk hunter had left me another gift. It was covered in dust and a little rust. At home, I had played with my dad's pocketknife and gotten in trouble for it. But this one was bigger and had a shiny blade, a screwdriver, and different blades that were can and bottle openers. I opened it up and shook the dust out of it, then put it in my pocket and felt rich. Now I had a pocketknife, and with it I could build a log cabin or take on any wild creature and win.

I had food, tools, and a shelter in the plastic tablecloth that I had not even used that night. I was ready for the mountains, ready for my day. I packed my backpack and sat on the hay bales, now in full sun, and ate my breakfast. Oreo cookies did not taste the same for breakfast. Too sweet. Too dry. Two cookies killed the hunger for a moment, but only made me thirstier.

If I had stayed in the Elk camp, rescuers would have found me rather quickly. But I still wanted to get to Iowa, even though I was really five hundred miles east of Iowa and I was headed south. To my left was a small trail leading down. I was tired of going up even though I was yet to hike that day. I followed the trail to a small spring fed brook. When I saw the clear water, without hesitation I dropped to my knees, stuck my face, and drank until I had the full feeling of a Thanksgiving dinner. Then I filled my water bottle, washed off my pocketknife, and began walking towards home, I thought.

I do not remember all the details of that day. I remember going up again. Being hot. Sweating. Eating Oreos. At one point, I found mushrooms. I had seen my parents eat mushrooms. They put them in spaghetti sauce and on salads. But I did not like mushrooms and could not talk myself into eating them. I later learned that would have been a fatal mistake. The mushrooms I had found were so poisonous that I would have died of kidney failure within 24 hours. I found berries, and while they were not ripe, they tasted good. But I only found nine or ten of them. Something else had already eaten them.

At one point I passed over another ridge, thinking it would be down to Iowa on the other side. But there were more mountains on the other side. Bigger mountains. Higher mountains. Once again, I went down a steep rockslide to a meadow, but this meadow did not have an elk camp, and as near as I could tell, it did not have water.

Pushing myself, I followed the slope down, across the meadow, then up, back into the trees. I liked these tall trees. I thought when I got to Iowa that I would suggest to the adults that they get trees like the ones in Wyoming. Tall. Green. Shade producing. An excellent home for critters.

It was getting late, and I expected the shadows of the trees to get longer again as the sun dipped over the ridge. But this time as the sun faded quickly and there was a deep roar as the wind whipped the tops of the trees, and they swayed back and forth. The clouds pushed in from the west in fast motion. They looked like they were just above the treetops, and they were dark, even black in places. My intuition took over. I started looking around for a place to shelter. There was no hay. No rock overhangs. Then the rain fell in heavy droplets began stinging me as they hit my bare head and arms.

Before I could take my pack off, my head was soaked and water was dripping down my back. I reached in my bag and pulled out my jacket, then grabbed the plastic tablecloth, tore it out of its wrapper, and pulled it around me. Instantly I found warmth as the wind no longer pierced through my thin clothes to my skin. I pulled my jacket hood on and it over my head and felt even less cold. Not warm, but less cold.

Among the deadfall, I found a large live fir tree. The tree's arms spread out like an umbrella, with the tips of the lower branches touching the ground. Underneath the tree was completely dry, with a bed of soft needles. I stepped into this natural shelter and found that the trunk of the tree was warm because the tree had spent the day in direct sun collecting heat. Grateful to have such a fine natural shelter, I pulled the plastic blanket around me, arranged my pack as a pillow, and placed my only light source, the toy car, within reach. Then I settled in for my second night in the woods alone. But this night was going to be nothing like my first night.

CHAPTER 7

The sun died, and the starless sky offered only darkness. I heard the uneven roar of the waves of rushing wind rising from the plains of Wyoming, pounding the sturdy tree that was my shelter. It reminded me of standing in the ocean at the beach and waiting for a wave to knock me off my feet. Every time a wave would hit, more needles would pour off the branches and onto my jacket and plastic cover. I could feel the stress of the wood fibers in my back as the tree swayed in the wind, but the anchored tree stayed true. I could not see the clouds anymore, but I could feel the motion of moisture moving above me. Occasionally, a lightning flash would reveal the sky that was just above the tip of the tree. A flash, and I would count, "One, alligator, two alligators, three alligators. Rumble. Three miles. The electricity, wind gusts and the clouds stirred my heart and chilled my bones. I felt cold gloom, then doom, and it got worse. Fear gusted into my core and opened wound. Flash. "One alligator. Two alligators. Rumble. Two miles. Panic seemed like it was creeping around my tree, always just out of sight, in the dark, stalking and waiting to pounce. Flash. One alligator. Rumble. One mile.

As my emotions and the storm synchronized, I questioned my plan and blamed myself for my predicament. Flash. One... Boom. The electric storm was on top of me. Flash. Boom again. Flash and crack. Between tears and torment, I placed my icy hands in my pocket and found more than warmth. I pushed them in harder, as if there might be more warmth deeper down, and felt the form of an old pocketknife. It had been there since I had cleaned it at the stream in the morning. I had not explored it, and now it was my only friend.

I took it out and placed it on my lap. It was larger than the palm of my hand, with a brown bone handle that made a sure adult size grip. I felt for the groove on the knife blade that gave my thumbnail the leverage to pull it open. It was stiff. Unused for a long time. I feared breaking my thumbnail. But just as the stressed nail was about to separate from the flesh, the hinge gave way and revealed a once shiny blade now spotted with tiny flakes of rust. This had not been a kid souvenir knife bought in a gift shop at a national park. It was a real pocketknife used for actual work, ranching, camping, and hunting. The blade was worn from being sharpened. I remember my father teaching me a little about knife care, so I looked around for a sandstone rock. I found a slightly pink stone at the edge of my protection ring that was flat on one side and put drops of water on it from the bottle. After passing the blade across a rock, grinding the flakes of rust away and leaving a blade that was shiny and sharp, I tested it on a stick, and the cut surprised me. But I had nothing that needed cutting. I cut anyway. Anything I could find. The knife brought me a sense of security that helped keep my fear at bay, under a tree, wrapped in a plastic tablecloth, in a thunderstorm at eight thousand feet. At least for now.

I opened the other tools on the knife. A smaller blade, also sharp after cleaning. A can opener and a bottle opener. I wished I had a can or a bottle. And a leather tool and a small saw blade. I tested the screwdriver, tightening the screws on the toy car. Using the gift, the pocketknife, brought me a sense of power, so much so that I cut a straight dead branch that was in the canopy above me. I whittled a point at one end of the stick, and drove it into the ground under the tree, then hung the plastic tablecloth over the dull end of the stick and made a teepee under the protective tree. I had two layers of protection now, with space to lie down.

But I did not stop there. I had learned something my first night. Grass, or hay, makes a pretty good mattress. The needles collected at the base of the tree were harder to manage, but they were dry, and they were the only thing within my eyesight that was dry. My plastic tablecloth makes a lousy blanket, but it was making a pretty good tent. Keeping out of the wind behind a warm tree trunk is the difference between just being cold and shivering uncontrollably. This was my camp. A pine needle bed, a plastic tablecloth, five remaining Oreo cookies, a toy police car with a glowing light, my pocketknife, and a worn-out grocery bag. A water bottle.

I dug a shallow trench in the pine needles downwind from the warm tree trunk and adjusted my plastic tent over my bed. The trench was just big enough that I could curl up in my jacket with my hood on to sleep. Pretty quickly, I realized it was going to be a hard night. The pine needles were a warm but uncomfortable mattress. The steady dripping from the tree branches made me realize I had to pee. Waiting until morning was not an option. After arguing with myself, I noticed that the thunder and lightning had moved further away, and the rain had stopped. In the space between the branches, I could see my way to the meadow and a place to do my business.

Once I stepped out from under the tree, it was not completely dark. Everything was the same shade of dark gray. This gave me confidence to go further from my camp. Further from the familiar. I walked fifty or one hundred feet. But when I turned around, when I was finished, the forest was a monotone gray. Every tree looked like every other tree. I could not see my path, and I was not sure which tree was my tree. The sky was opening. The rain began again, only this time without wind, hard and direct. Now I was doubly lost. Lost in the wilderness and lost in the woods. Lost in these mountains, miles from a road. And lost from my camp, 30 or 40 steps away.

At this moment, the emotional free fall returned, and in my private storm that buffeted my head and heart, I acknowledged I was not headed to Iowa. Iowa was not just over the next ridge. I was not headed home. I did not know where I was headed. I did not know where my pine needle bed was.

Panic started in my lower stomach and moved up my rib cage into my throat. I knew if I let it out my mouth that I would drop to my knees, fall on my face, and be done. I could not let that happen. No. Focus. I was 20 to 30 steps away, in the dark. But what exact direction? I retraced my last five steps, then saw the deadfall I had stepped over. Now I was closer. My eyes scanned the growing darkness. Every tree looked like a black photocopy of the one next to it. I picked a direction and counted off twenty steps, then looked again, but nothing was familiar. Panic rose again. But I found a powerful way to fight the panic. Guilt.

"Stupid me!" I shouted. "Idiot!" I called myself every bad word I had ever heard. It did not make me feel better, but it kept the panic at the bottom of my stomach. Not wanting to go too far, and not wanting to go in the wrong direction, I walked in circles. Each time around I went a little further out, keeping the deadfall I had stepped over on my left and walking counterclockwise. Nothing seemed familiar. Nothing was right. I sat down on a log and invited the panic in. It was over. I was done for. Bad to worse. Abandoned. Doomed.

One step further. I'll go one step further along this log. One step turned into two, then three. It was completely dark now. Just a band of quiet light along the horizon. There was a flash of lightning in the distance, and at the same instance, a subtle reflection at the base of one tree, just ten feet in front of me. Was I imagining it? The flash and reflection came again as I took one step towards it. Yes, the reflection was coming from the knife blade I had cleaned and left open and stabbed in the tree bark in my shelter. Five steps and I felt the plastic tablecloth below my feet. I was home. I was no longer lost. I recaptured a small portion of my dignity, then I felt around for the toy car, and pressed the top. The small red light came on. With my little bubble of light, I centered on the sleeping place, and pulled my feet up to my chest, and my now wet jacket around me until I was completely under my fragile plastic tent. The light from the toy car defined my space and seemed to make things a little warmer, so I kept my finger on the top until the batteries weakened, and my grip failed, and sleep relieved me from my fears.

I woke during the night to find the panic in my stomach trying to rise again. Once, I got up to take a leak, but as I rose off the bed and out from under the plastic, I was assaulted by the cold. I took a half step away from my bed and relieved myself quickly, then tried in vain to recover the little warmth that I had stored. Before long, my teeth were chattering, and with the physical misery came the feelings of being lost, alone, and helpless. It was the only time in my life when I can remember crying myself to sleep.

During the night, the sky cleared a little and my little cocoon became warmer. Through the branches above me, through the plastic, I could see the stars being erased by a line of clouds. Then the wind, a big wind, bending the little tree. There were flashes of lightning, then thunder. When the wind died, big rain drops penetrated the sheltering branches and hit me on my plastic tent. So, I pulled the tablecloth down and wrapped it around my body, capturing what little warmth my core was generating. Then I pulled my head underneath the plastic carefully, so I could take in the outside air, but breathe the warm air my body was generating. The rain came in bursts, but I was mostly protected in my pit of pine needles. In the early hours of the morning, I drifted off to a solid sleep.

CHAPTER 8

I was used to being awakened by sound. In Iowa, an alarm clock shattered my dreams every morning and reminded me I was in the real world. But this morning, I was awakened by smell. Not harsh. Not sweet. But fresh. The clean smell of chilly air filtered by nature. As my nose slowly came alive again, my heart was at peace. When they were ready, my ears followed my nose into consciousness. There were sounds of a forest alive. The symphony again, only different. Different birds. Louder, bolder birds. Then the insects, like the rhythm section of an orchestra. Then squirrels. The off-key soloists. Off, somewhere in the distance, the string section of water running and a breeze turning leaves in the trees. Sounds that made the background of the gentile welcome back to reality.

I was fully awake enough to know that being fully awake would mean facing my situation. But then my fatigue captured me again. I needed more sleep. I finally slept soundly as the world was reborn, then woke to the warm, bright sunshine that was heating my little shelter. With the sun, the birds were no longer singing, but I could hear the low hum of bugs in the grass and trees, and an occasional warning chirp from a chipmunk or squirrel. I was awake in the real world. Hunger burned my stomach. Thirst twisted my tongue. I rubbed my mouth, and where my lips had been, something that felt like unfinished cement. My still tired eyes scanned the landscape. I was no longer looking for signs of Iowa. I was looking for signs of civilization. Anything that was made by humans. A trail, a road, anything. I tried to whistle, but all I could do was flap my lips in an embarrassing sound. I called out.

"Hey! (pause) I need help," I called in a weak voice, but in a brave admission. Even though I was completely alone, I felt self-conscious. I waited and heard nothing. I called again, and again, but my appeal could not penetrate my little space. So, I walked across the little field where I had been lost the night before, and I called out again. I could see where I had been, where I had walked in circles, and was ashamed of how clear things were in the light. Now it was clear that I needed help, but my voice was spent. I kept walking, even though my belongings were in the grocery bag in my shelter, but told myself I would not be long. Besides, I had my most cherished knife in my pocket. I would not need the other things because I hoped I would quickly see a trail, a hiker, or someone nearby looking for me. Yet somewhere deep inside, a voice was telling me the truth of my situation. I was completely alone and disconnected. There was nothing or no one nearby. I was a long way from home and a long way from Lincoln, Wyoming. But I could not face that reality, so I engaged in self-deception and told myself that help was near.

The other voice, not the truth voice, doubted someone would look for me, but it was wrong. Aunt Marge was thinking I would turn up, and she was busy gossiping with her friends. Billy was glad he did not have to share his room. Mom and Dad were busy "working out their issues," and didn't even know I was gone. The people in the church picnic would surely search for one of their own, but they would not search for me. I remembered the story of the "Good Samaritan." The point of the story was to remind people to help strangers. I was not part of their clan, and unless they were reminded, they would not search for me.

I began searching myself, looking for anything that would help. After walking just a short distance, I noticed the edge of the field sloped down to a row of trees, and just inside the trees there was the rushing water of the small stream I had heard. I assured myself I was not dreaming, then rushed to the water. Sliding to the edge of the stream on my knees, I pushed my face into the current, and felt the cold, sweet liquid on my lips, and cheeks, my tongue. "Thank you," my heart spoke to an unknown creator. "Thank you for giving me this stream in my moment of need." For a moment, just a moment, I felt like someone was standing by me.

The brook was only ankle deep and ran over gravel and small rocks. There was no moss, no green slime. Just clear, cold water. This stream was the headwaters of the river I had crossed near the picnic grounds. Down there the runoff choked river was much bigger, and in places moving fast enough to knock you off your feet. Down there, you had to stay on the boulders or get washed away. On the back eddies and slow places, it was plugged with moss. It was like a playground bully and best to stay clear of. But this stream was my friend. Calm. Not threatening.

I lay on my stomach in the grass by the shore with my head over the water. I drank my fill. The chilly water brought life again to my lips and instant relief to my parched mouth and throat. And it dulled the hunger that pulsed in my belly. I splashed water on my face and felt a sting and a comfort at the same time. My fingers turned brown at the touch of my face, and I realized it must be very dirty. So, I leaned down next to the freezing water, cupped my hands, and washed my face, hair, and neck until the surrounding water was brown and muddy from the dust I was carrying.

I leaned back and lay in the grass, looking up at the clouds. At that moment, I saw this space differently. It was a blessing, and I felt rich and happy. Then I rolled over in the grass and lay on my side. The effects of the freshwater worked their way into my dehydrated system. I needed more water and something to eat. As I was planning my second drinking, just lying in the grass, my eye caught something in the grass. Something red and small. It was not moving. It was not alive. At least in the sense of a bug, it was not alive. I focused on the red against green grass and realized I was seeing a tiny, very ripe strawberry. It was about the size of my fingernail. I picked it and gulped it without inspection. It was sour even though it was fully ripe. I quickly looked for more, ripe and or not, and ate as quickly as possible. The tiny berries had tiny seeds and tiny stems. If I pulled the stems off, like you did with real strawberries, then there was not much left. So, I ate the stems too, then drank again.

The two dozen wild strawberries I found in 20 minutes of searching, plus the water, put a small but helpful dent in my hunger. But it also gave me confidence. A sense of self-sufficiency. I was warm, fed, and rested. The warm sun was at my back as I walked back into the field. I didn't have fire, but I didn't think I needed fire, and I really did not know how to use fire. For a moment, I thought I might live in this place. I would eat Oreos and wild strawberries and sleep under a tree in the pine needles every night. No school. No friends, but then I didn't have any friends. No Billie and Aunt Marge and fighting parents. It would be a good life.

Then I saw the flash, a mile off in the distance. A silvery light from a shiny object. An undefined piece of civilization. It flashed from a treetop, or behind it. I could not tell. Was it a window on a house? A car? A sign? It was flashing at me. But it was just a random flash. It was just below another ridge top, looking down at me away and up, through dense trees and brush. To get to it, I needed to cross the field and cross a patch of thick brush. I had been stuck in that kind of thick brush a few times in the last few days. The direct approach would not work. To the left, I could see a steep but clear route going up to the ridge. It was rocky, but clear of the dense brush that would envelop me if I took the direct approach. Once on the ridge, I could look down at the light source and see what it was.

Crossing the field, and strengthened by the hope that civilization was nearby, I did not go back to the backpack or the plastic tablecloth that was at the other end of the meadow in my little shelter. I had my knife, and hopefully soon I would be sitting at McDonald's with a burger, telling my story to an interested third party.

But halfway across the field, I had a strange feeling that can only be described by the cliché of having "the hair on the back of my neck stand up." Someone or something was watching me. I looked up at the flashing light that would occasionally catch the sun, but that was not it.

It was something closer. Dangerous, perhaps, but not aggressive. It was watching me, but I was not watching it because I did not know what "it" was. But I knew "it" was watching me. When I was younger, I would give into my fears, fear of darkness, fear of being alone, fear of being watched. In this case, I was not afraid, just vigilant. I knew it was there. I was in its space, and it was time to leave.

Part of me was proud that I was understanding, even feeling my surroundings. I had found food. I had found water, and even made shelter. I knew my environment. I did not own my environment. But I shared it with other creatures, other living things. And they shared theirs with me. Water, berries, warm tree trunks, pine needles. But my pride came bundled in new fears. I was being watched. Someone or something knew where I was and what I was doing, and I knew nothing about them. I stopped walking. I looked around. A quick scan at first, then a long, 360-degree turn, studying every bush, every shadow, every tree. I saw nothing, but the feeling of being watched intensified.

I continued across the field, passed through trees, and climbed up the steep side of the ridge. As I climbed, the sun stung the exposed back of my neck, my feet felt worn and blistered, and I quickly became thirsty again. With these distractions, the sense of being watched slowly went away. The step brush slope became rocky. And the rocky became boulders. The boulders were like steps for someone twelve feet tall, so I had to drag myself up and over in some places. Still, it was easier than going through the dense brush that covered the other part of the slope. The higher I got, the more excited I became, wondering what my discovery would be. A phone booth? Never mind that I did not have a coin and most phone booths were no longer maintained. Perhaps a weather station, or a beacon? A fire lookout? A highway sign? No. I would have seen or heard cars. A cabin.

The sun was now directly overhead, and the effect of my long drinks and small meal was wearing off. I was thirsty again, and my hunger that had gone into hiding after the strawberries had returned with a vengeance. After climbing around a difficult boulder, I rested, turned around, and dangled my feet. I looked back on where I had traveled, down on the field, and I could see my track in the shine in the matted grass where I had crossed. I followed my track back to the edge of the stream, then gazed up to my evergreen camp at the other end.

Then, in the shadows of the trees at the opposite end of the field, I saw a large, deep brown motionless creature. It was sitting in the grass, so its eyes were level with the top of the tall grass. Its antlers, which looked like tree branches, blended into the background. I had walked within 150 feet of it, right towards it. As I watched, it rose, awkwardly pulling its gangly legs under its massive body. Once all four feet were planted under its head and rack, it walked gracefully through the grass to where I had crossed the meadow, then turned towards the stream and away from me, and walked towards the water. The moose stopped and drank, then ate grass. It turned its head towards my camp, and not liking what it smelled, took three steps in the opposite direction into the shadows of the trees and was gone.

Wow. I did not see the moose, yet I was within charging range. But I had felt it and had completely believed what my senses were telling me. I did not stand a chance if it had charged, but it had not tried to harm me or even scare me. I wondered if anyone would believe me when I told this story. Anyone. I needed to get back to civilization if I was going to tell this story to someone. So, I pulled my legs back over the boulder, turned, and continued up the boulder field.

Just below the ridgeline the boulders became a small cliff, and my only option was to bushwhack around the cliff. It took a half hour to go the last fifty feet in a patch of thick brush that scratched my arms like a cornered barn cat. The going was slow, but finally I broke out onto the panoramic ridge. I could look down behind me on the empty meadow, home to the moose. I could see the small stream and my camp at the far end. Up over the rise, I could see much more.

I could see all of Lincoln County and beyond. Out over the plains to the horizon. There was a haze over the expanse, but I could clearly see where the wilderness ended and civilization began. Below me, I could see where my stream joined another and then another and became the river that I had crossed on the picnic grounds. I could see roads and fields, and the hill where I had started. The wilderness presented directly below me, and bigger, rugged mountains above me, and I realized I had come a long way, through a hard country, and that Iowa, or Colorado, was not up here. I only hoped to find the source of the reflection and use it to take me home.

CHAPTER 9

The spine of the ridge top was rocky, but bare, so moving up towards the source of the sometimes-reflecting light was easy. But now I was at the wrong angle to see the reflection, so I kept moving along the ridge and looking. I knew it was below me, but I could not pinpoint the location. It was just below the ridge, but not obvious from this angle. At some point, I realized I had gone too far. I must have passed it. It was not a road or a trail, or a building. It was a small and annoying mystery that I could no longer see. For a moment I wondered if I had really seen anything, but then I shifted back to trusting myself. I had felt the moose, and I had seen the reflection. I went back down the ridge, cutting into the large group of trees where I expected to see the shiny object. But nothing. I looked up and down.

Disappointed, I sat and rested in the shade at the base of a tree. I must be close. Through the tree branches I could see the field, and I was just below the ridge where I had seen it. It was late afternoon, and the wind picked up sending shivers through the trees. My ears filtered the wind noise and found something artificial. A crinkly sound like what you got when you wadded up a piece of paper or plastic. I looked up. My ears lead my eyes to the sound. Strings. Plastic. Foil. No mylar. At the top of one tree, I saw a dozen deflated balloons tied together. The old fashion balloons were long gone, but the strings were still flapping in the wind. The three mylar balloons were deflated, and almost new looking. They rattled and crinkled in the wind and occasionally caught the sunlight and flashed. One of them said, "Happy Birthday Leo" on the other side. Another had once been the shape of a number. I studied it. Yes. The number nine. I was nine years old, and this garbage set adrift in the sky, set by helium gas, was playing a cruel trick on me. Lost birthday balloons had drifted for miles, hundreds of miles, until the trees in these mountains caught them. Besides, I had just spent the better part of the day thinking this would save me.

I wanted to be angry, but I had no one to be angry with. So, I went emotionally numb. I knew I could not go over the ridge toward where I thought I would find a road, a city, civilization and/or Iowa. The terrain was too rugged for me. That used to be no big deal. In my ordeal, I had become a realist. I could not backtrack to civilization, at least not without food and water, and much-needed rest. I could only go back to the stream, back to the field, back to my camp, and settle in for another night.

Going down was harder than going up. I clawed the bushes and fingered the boulders to lower myself safely, cutting surface wounds on my fingers and palm. I worked against gravity on the way up. On the way down, gravity was too much my willing friend. Twice I fell, and both times I scraped something that later needed washing and cleaning with the handy wipes in my pack. The pain in my knees was not as strong as the hunger pain in my stomach. When I stopped, my hands trembled, and my legs felt weak. I was running out of gas.

When I finally got to the meadow, I headed straight for the stream and drank. Then I cleaned the scratches on my arms and the scrapes on my knees. Cleaning the wounds brought stabbing pain, but it only lasted seconds. Then I drank again. I looked for wild strawberries along the ground but found none. Then I remembered the bull moose and wondered if he was still around. My senses told me he was not, but I could see his tracks where he had crossed the stream earlier in the day. I went back, across the field, to camp and found my backpack, undisturbed and waiting. I ate three of the five remaining Oreo cookies, then took the water bottle, returned to the stream, and filled it with water. Then I spent my last energy grabbing armfuls of dead grass dried in the day's sunlight and laying in patches around the meadow. I put half the stack over the pine needles where I had slept and kept half for a blanket.

I settled into the shelter before sundown, still stinging from my disappointment and wasted day. I had no idea what I would do tomorrow. The immediate future was a monster I could not face. The grass, the deadfall logs, the plastic tablecloth, the water bottle that would have been garbage to me two days ago, my toy police car with the now burned-out light, two Oreo cookies, my jacket, the handy wipes, and my knife, the blade that gave me protection, these were all that I had. My disappointment turned, and I was grateful for having so much.

CHAPTER 10

Blood caked on the raw wounds on my arms. My muscles ached. The cookies had put a dent in my hunger, and the water bloated my belly. I lay on the grass pile mattress, unwilling to move anymore, but too tired to sleep. I lay looking at the meadow through the branch canopy, hoping that the moose would return, and waiting for the devil of darkness to descend. Soon the shadows of the trees got longer, the temperature began to drop, and my spiraling spirits began to descend as well. In the growing shadows, my fears were again stalking me. My dried lips, scabbing arms, and empty belly were forgotten. Even the chill of the evening took a back seat to the doom that haunted my little boy heart. I wanted to go home. I wanted mom. I wanted dad. I wanted my bed. My pillow. My place. I even wanted Aunt Marge, and Billy. I wanted anyone who knew my name.

As I stared into the growing twilight, my eyes let go of the shadows, and I raised my head upwards, to the sunless sky. I remembered how blessed I had felt by the stream that morning, and how gratitude had chased disappointment from my heart that evening. The feathery clouds furled around the pink horizon where the remnants of blue sky and red mixed in colors and tones that had no names. For the first time in my life, I felt both fear and an overwhelming sense of beauty. Such a wonderful and deadly world. Such a full and empty place that filled my a grateful and devastated heart.

I did not know how to pray. Oh, yes. I had heard Aunt Marge and others give a "blessing on the food" and casually talk to God like he was their BFF on Facebook. I had seen TV preachers raise their hands up and shout at God. But this sky, and this darkness and these raw emotions gave me different feelings about God. About sacredness. While I felt small and insignificant, I could also see the immense value of my creation. I knew the importance of my life, and I wanted to live it. I wanted the joy and the disappointment that life would bring in the form of surprises.

God was with me and distant. He was in the stars or beyond, but he also was close, even right next to me. Like I could touch his face, and he could touch mine. Not in the trees, or even sitting next to me. Sitting with me. "Hey God," I said. "I want to live." "Please, God. I want to live."

I said it again. And again. "I want to live, God." Not like I was angry and demanding, but like I was talking to a friend. Then I said, "Hey God, thanks for mom and dad, and Aunt Marge, and everyone. Thanks for this sky. Thanks for the chilly water. For the pocketknife. Thanks for the warm bed. "This world is cool." It was at that moment that the magnetic poles of my world shifted. Things like parental conflict, running away, living with strange relatives were now insignificant problems. Finding home, finding civilization, finding myself, was a big problem. A scary problem. A problem that I was facing, but no longer alone.

I lay there afraid of my own tears and feeling faith for the first time in my life. In moments, before the shadows in the trees turned into monsters, I was asleep.

In minutes, or hours, I don't know when; I awoke in complete blackness, feeling again that someone or something was watching me. I listened to my instincts. The moose? No. It was close, but I was afraid to look. To face the creature. Then I really heard it. Paws moving slowly in my direction. I felt for the knife. In the layers of black, I could see movement but no shape. I had studied animals in my favorite first grade book "Animals of the Rocky Mountains." It's not a bear. A wolf or a mountain lion? I opened the pocketknife blade and pointed it in the sound's direction. My eyes tried to focus on the dark, shapeless movement. For a flashing moment, its eyes caught light from somewhere. It was crawling towards me slowly. My fingers tightened around the pocketknife, but it brought no real comfort. Then with my left hand I pressed the top of the toy car, hoping for just a tiny light so I could see my enemy. The brief and dying red glow momentarily pierced the darkness and created a small light bubble around me. My eyes had not adjusted to the light, but I could see the creature pause, its nose on the ground. It was seeing me with its nose. Stalking me and just inches from my extended feet, I instinctively pulled them into the little red-light bubble, hoping the light would protect me. All I could see was its nose following my feet into the light. In the distorted red light, and my still sleepy eyes, I could see it was blonde like a mountain lion but had an enormous nose like a wolf. It did not growl or seem angry. Or hungry. It just smelled me, turned, and ran away. Into the darkness, away from the field.

At first, I was relieved. The threat was gone. Then I remembered wolves hunted in packs. It was going to get the pack. I would be breakfast for the wolf pups that were too young to hunt. My fears raged. Should I climb the tree? Should I fight back with my stick? My knife? Should I run? It was too dark for anything. No moon or stars. No light on the horizon. After a while, my exhaustion overcame my fears, and I floated off to half sleep again.

I don't know how long I slept, but again I awoke with the feeling that I was being watched. This time I stood up to face my adversary, busting through the plastic tablecloth with my back to the tree. The battery and light on the toy car were spent. I could see a dim light in the sky forming on the horizon. My plastic tablecloth blanket drifted to the surrounding ground. The creature again stepped into my space, and this time came even closer. I felt its breath on my toes, knees, legs. "Don't look. Don't make eye contact." I remembered the cautions from my animal book. So, I looked straight ahead. Then its cold nose touched the hand that was holding the knife, just above my clenched fist, and it turned and was gone again. In the slowly dying darkness, I could see it running back the way it came with purpose. This time I could see a large, bushy tail silhouetted in the graying sky.

I stood there shaking for the cold, for the release of fear, for the feelings of helplessness. I was afraid to move, but I reached down and picked up the tablecloth and pulled it around me like a blanket. Still, I was afraid to lie down. Afraid to eat my last two Oreos. The light, now pink, on the horizon gradually spilled into the forest. I could make out the trees and the deadfall around the shrinking shadows. The morning birds were singing. A squirrel chirped a warning sound, and then the birds went silent. The creature was back. This time, I could see it coming from afar. It was weaving between trees and deadfall, gracefully leaping over logs, but clearly coming for me. Before I knew what it was, before I could really see its features, its face, its paws, something happened that was a complete surprise. I was no longer afraid.

. . .

The bell rang. Once again, I was sitting in front of the class, deep into an unfinished story. I reached into my pocket and pulled out the little red car with the red light. The paint was worn, and the wheels in front were missing, and the light still did not work. Instantly, and without invitation, my fellow students stepped forward. They touched it, picked it up, and passed it around. Everyone tested the light. Then I took out my treasure. My knife. It had been cleaned and sharpened since my ordeal, but still worn with experience. I carried it everywhere except to school. The boys in the class now crowded around my chair and each wanted to touch it.

I looked at Mr. White, who had an ear-to-ear grin on his face. I had never seen a serious teacher, a respected teacher, a sometimes-feared teacher, but mostly loved by students' teacher smile like that. He looked around the class and he knew it was working. "Let's give Caleb one more day to finish this up." No one disagreed. Emily shot him a deliberate smile. The cool guy held up his hand for a "high five." I hit it hard. "Nice job, Cowboy," he said, like we had been friends forever. Students coming in early for the next period looked at our lingering class with envy. They could feel the energy and wished, hoped, it would spill into their class, too.

Mr. White came over and put his arm around me. He took the knife, and in an apologetic tone he said, "I gotta take this until school is over. It violates school policy to have knives, and I don't want you to get in trouble. If you did, we might not get to hear the end of this story." His smile continued. "You can trust me to keep this safe until seventh period." He smiled and pointed me towards the door. "Now don't be late for your next class."

PART II: FOUND

CHAPTER 11

Aunt Marge let out a scream that rattled the picnic grounds like an earthquake that was 9.8 on the Richter scale. This was not a "I've seen a snake" scream, or an "I've had enough of you kids" scream. This was a scream that came from a person whose life went from happy to horror in a nanosecond. It communicated fear and guilt, horror, and helplessness, all wrapped into one earth shaking ear shattering bellow. It penetrated the trees and the vehicles and turned heads, so the screamer had everyone's attention in an instant.

The preacher's wife was walking across the rutted half-paved parking lot when she heard the scream. The shock wave of sound caused her to drop a big bowl of left-over potato salad onto the dusty tarmac, sending the mustard and mayo mixture into a miniature mushroom cloud that plastered on the door panels of nearby trucks and cars. This was her prized culinary contribution to the picnic. Everyone said they liked it, but she noticed that the dense mixture was still on the floppy paper plates when they were placed in the trash, and now the rest of it was melting the paint of the Plymouth minivan and the old ranch truck. The preacher tiptoed through the puddle of spuds and mayo to find Marge leaning on her car door with Billy sitting white faced in the back seat.

"He's gone!" she told the man. "Gone!" "The little boy is gone!" In her panic, she could not remember Caleb's name.

The preacher looked at Billy, then looked at Marge, then looked at Billy again. "He's right here," he said in an artificially calm voice he had learned in preacher school. "Right here in the back seat."

Marge looked at the preacher like he was a major league buffoon. Then she looked at Billy and hollered in a raspy voice laden with more fear than anger, "He's gone. That, that boy. Caleb." Pointing to the empty seat next to Billy.

"I thought he was with Billy. I thought he was playing around. But he's gone. Gone!" she said, gulping air between every phrase.

By then the preacher's wife, with her shoes covered with a sick-looking mud of yellow mayo, was standing next to the preacher.

"Who's gone?" they both said at the same time.

Marge ignored the question, speaking to an imaginary crowd. "He's gone. Vanished. Poof!"

The preacher said, "Let's calm down." The preacher's wife echoed, "Calm down." Billy rolled his eyes. After a series of "calm downs," she focused on Marge and said, "What's wrong, honey?"

"What's wrong? What's wrong?" Marge could not find the volume control on her voice and everyone who was still in the parking lot could hear her every word. Even people in downtown Lincoln that was three-and-a-half miles away could hear every word. "My niece brought her son to live with me and I've lost him. In less than 24 hours, I've lost him."

Then she buried her head in her hands and began a dramatic cry that was mostly sincere, but still partly for show.

Billy used this as his cue and said in a calm, indifferent voice, "No one has seen Caleb for two hours. He's nine-years-old, and he wants to go back to Iowa." Realizing that he had everyone's attention, he added in a sarcastic voice, "He has a bad attitude." Billy echoed a phrase he had heard a thousand times about himself. This was his chance to try it out on someone else.

The preacher's wife pivoted, looked at the river running through the park, assumed the worst, and screamed. It was the 9.2 aftershock to Marge's first earthquake, reverberating off the cars and trailers still in the parking lot. Suddenly, everyone froze in their places. It was one thing to have Marge scream, but the preacher's wife. An off-duty sheriff's deputy named Mike, who was cleaning up from the softball game, was already moving toward the mayhem. That's just what law enforcement people do. He approached and asked the right questions, learning that a nine-year-old named Caleb was seen walking towards the stream with a grocery bag when the party was just starting. He had not been seen since. Mike quickly headed towards the stream. As he walked down the path, he could see a young man, thirteen, holding hands with a young girl. Mike interrupted the "first kiss" moment, and the two let go of each other's hands like they were holding poison ivy. They explained themselves, but Mike interrupted with an urgent voice, telling them that a nine-year-old boy was missing. Relieved that the screaming and related fuss was not about them, the young boy told Mike that they had been put in charge of keeping kids out of the stream.

"Once I had to yell at this kid," said the young man as if he had done his job perfectly. "The kid turned right around and scurried back to the party," he said in a voice slightly lower than his regular speaking voice.

Then the young woman interrupted. "No," she said. "No, you yelled at him, but then you kept right on talking to me. You didn't watch him. I'm sure you had your back turned. You watched me. We didn't see where he went, right? She looked at the boy who was expected to have to confess his negligence to this sheriff's deputy."

Quickly, Mike moved to the stream, where he saw only one set of footprints in the little sandy bar. They were fresh, little footprints that looked like they had come from a nine-year-old who had crossed the sand leading to the boulders and stepped into the swift water. He assumed the worst. This was where the boy had gone into the water. If he had looked more closely, he would have seen that the last footprint, just at the edge of the water, was more pronounced. It went deeper into the sand because the boy planted his foot and launched himself onto a boulder.

He quickly felt for his cell phone and dialed the sheriff's dispatcher.

"Sally, we got into a situation here at the church picnic. Better call out search and rescue and tell them to rig for a water search. Get everyone going if you can. We've got a nine-year-old boy who went in the water about two hours ago and he has not been seen since."

Mike then took out his phone and took pictures of the footprints to preserve them as evidence. Within an hour, there would be a whole lot of people working in the water. While he was using his phone as a camera, the urgent text message from the Lincoln County Search and Rescue Team came out.

"All SAR members. Search for a missing 9 YO M. Rotary Picnic Area near Lincoln. Rig for water search."

Then Mike returned to the parking lot where the preacher, the preacher's wife, and Aunt Marge were standing in a circle. It was hard to tell who was crying and who was comforting. By then, dogs were happily cleaning the potato salad off the side of the cars.

In his command voice, Mike interrupted and said, "I need everyone's help. First, Marge, take Billy home and stay by the phone, in case the boy went home with the wrong people, and they call you." Everyone in Lincoln knew Marge was the only person in the county that still used her landline. This also got Marge out of the area if they found the body in the water.

"Second," he pointed to the preacher's wife, "I need you to get people to search every vehicle still in this parking lot and in the grass about the park. Search the bathrooms, bleachers, and any place he might be asleep or hiding. Then he pointed to the preacher. "I need you to get five or six men, older men, to come with me. We are going to search quickly along the river."

Mike knew that keeping them busy with something important to do would help them deal with the horror of losing a child. The men gathered just below the rocks where Mike had seen the footprints and told the men to follow the river, or stream, or whatever it was down to the bridge, about a half mile.

"Stay away from the current. We don't want anyone else in the water. Just look to see if the boy had gotten out of the water or was hanging onto something. Hurry," he said.

Then he stepped to his car that bore the markings "Lincoln County Sheriff." With the windows up, he pulled the microphone off the dashboard clip, paused, and said, "Central, 1J345."

"This is Central," he heard Sally's voice. He went formal, professional with his voice because he knew if this went big that the communications recording would be listened to by the new sheriff and other investigators assessing the response.

"Sally," he paused. "I mean central," he corrected. "Is Nate, I mean Deputy Nate Garner, on duty? We're going to need Boo."

"He just went off duty from a 12-hour shift," she said.

"Well, let's let him rest for a few hours, then get him going before the big push in the morning," he said. "If we are still searching in the morning," he added, knowing that they would.

CHAPTER 12

Deputy Nate Garner slept through the first three phone calls. On the fourth call, Sally was about ready to send an officer over to his house, but all officers were on their way to Rotary Club Park to look for a missing kid. She was glad when the fourth call woke him from a deep sleep that he had been enjoying for just 15 minutes. Nate had heard a search and rescue call out just as he was going off duty, but he figured it would be like most missing kid calls. The boy would be found asleep in the grass or in the back seat of a car.

Sally was not her usual cheery self, full of pleasantries. "Nate?" she asked in a professional tone. It was his first clue that whatever was going on was important.

"What do you need?" he asked.

"Mike and the sheriff want you to bring Boo up to Rotary Park picnic ground on the Lincoln River. It seems like there is a missing nine-year-old who might be in the river."

"It's hardly a river," Nate said in a grumpy voice. Sally, the dispatcher countered, "It's running high right now. I'd call it a river for the next two weeks."

"Alright." Nate hung up and leaned over to kiss Marie, his wife. He pulled on his pants, which he strangely kept on his nightstand, found his cleanest sheriff's deputy shirt, and put on his hiking boots. Then he went to kiss Marie who should have been in the bed next to him. During his dressing, she had slipped into the kitchen and was preparing a takeaway breakfast and a lunch for his backpack. She knew the routine.

Nate was half conscious, still exhausted from a twelve on and twelve off the day before. He passed through the kitchen, kissing Marie on the back of her neck. "Thanks, Hon," he said. She forced a smile. Nate knew she would stay up and listening to the police scanner until he was home.

He grabbed his service revolver, his hiking pack, and Boo's vest that said "Search and Rescue" on the side. It was his uniform, and like people, when he put his uniform on, he knew he was working. Back in the kitchen, he could see the time on the microwave read 4:32 AM. Marie had filled a water bottle for him, one for Boo, and one for the potential subject, or an unprepared searcher. He took his red search pack off a peg, and his hand-held radio off the charger. He then took a spare battery out of the drawer and put it in his search pack. All the time he could hear Boo whining and pushing against the door. The dog knew what was coming.

There was another low energy kiss for Marie. Both were still in a sleep deprived state. As he pressed the automatic garage door opener, then opened the door to the backyard, he said just loud enough to not wake the neighbors, "Boo! Let's go to work." Like a bullet, Boo shot through the gate and onto the back bumper of the truck, then in through the open window of the shell. "Nothing should have that much energy at this hour," he thought, as he stumbled towards the truck, searching for his enthusiasm. In the back of the truck, he could see Boo, who turned and faced his master with a big, bushy tail that slapped the side of the truck, and a dangling tongue that made him look like he was always smiling.

Boo was a 4-year-old Golden Retriever certified search dog.

"Good boy," Nate said in the same tone he always did. He made the two words sound like one. Boo lived for praise even when he did routine things right. "Let's go to work," he reached in and scratched the head of the dog. Boo nudged his wrist and relished the touch. Nate dumped his back in the back of the truck, then shut the rear window to keep the dust from the dirt roads from covering his gear and his dog.

Before he could get in the cab. Boo had unlatched the window, and it popped open. Boo had learned to place his paw on the latch cable in just the right way to open the window and cool down the cabin. There was no use in closing it again.

Nate stepped into the driver's side of his Lincoln County Sheriff's department truck and started the engine. As he pulled out of the garage, now fully awake, he pulled the radio microphone off the clip and spoke in a tired voice. "Sally…" He corrected himself. He remembered the new sheriff wanted them to use a more professional radio protocol. "Central, this is 1J747. Please show me in route to Rotary Park. Do they want me to pick up donuts?" Sally came on. "1J747, Central. Negative on the donuts. The search is becoming urgent. 4:35 AM."

When dispatch said "urgent," Nate flipped on his light bar and pressed the gas pedal. He cut the ten-minute drive down to seven and pulled into the dusty parking lot that was filling up with emergency vehicles and search and rescue volunteers. People with bright green/yellow shirts were pulling on their search packs or getting into wetsuits.

Nate called dispatch and reported he was on scene, then he climbed out of his truck, grabbed his hand-held radio, put on his search pack, and stepped out of the cab. Boo followed. The sheriff was standing with Mike next to a car, with a hand-held radio in one hand and a map of the river in the other, while older volunteers were still setting up a mobile command post nearby. "Hi Nate," Mike said, as he approached. The sheriff said stiffly, "Thanks for coming, Deputy Garner. Deputy Rich has an assignment for you and your K-9." The sheriff did not know the difference between professionalism and being formal. So, he never used first names. Everyone was addressed by rank. Dogs were "K-9s." Cars were "vehicles." And your neighbors who you sat next to in church on Sunday were subjects, victims, persons of interest, or part of the law enforcement family.

Mike stepped up and showed Nate the clipboard. "I tracked him to the edge of the water right here. The river is running high right now. We sent a hasty team along the banks downstream from the point-last-seen, and we have another team getting ready to work in the river in wetsuits, working downstream."

"So, this is the PLS?" Nate pointed to the place on the map where the stream and the picnic grounds merged. PLS is the common term searchers use of the "point last seen." It is where every search begins.

"Yes," said Mike. "A couple of teenagers saw him near the river right there. We want you to work downstream as fast as you can ahead of the team that will be in dry suits in the river and see if you can find him. It's too late for good news. He's been gone almost seven hours, or more."

"Do you have a scent article?" Nate asked. He could see that the sheriff was annoyed. He wanted Nate to get working quickly. Images of searchers in the parking lot were not what the sheriff wanted the public to see. He wanted to show the press that K-9s were currently involved in the search. He wanted Nate to provide a photo opportunity because he thought dogs were just good for the cameras. People solved problems, not dogs. Nate pressed. "I need something with his scent on it, so Boo knows who he is looking for. Otherwise, he will just find the other searchers."

Mike had thought of that ahead of time, so before Marge had left, he had put on rubber gloves, taken gauze pads from the first aid kit, and ran it over the seat where Caleb had been sitting. This collected the skin rafts, microscopic pieces of dead skin humans are constantly shedding that have a person's unique signature. This would give Boo a picture of who he was looking for. Humans might like a paper picture of who they are looking for. Dogs want a smell. Mike had carefully placed the gauze in a plastic bag so as not to contaminate it with his own scent. "Got you covered," Mike told Nate. The sheriff looked surprised when Mike produced the bag with the "scent article" from his briefcase. "I'll get going," Nate said.

"With Boo on his lead, Nate headed through the picnic area. Boo had already picked up the emotion of the search, playing on the excitement of the situation. He walked tall and undistracted through the crowd, like he knew the real meaning of professionalism. Boo could smell the emotions of humans. He knew this was real and not training. He put his own senses on alert, and as they passed through the picnic ground, he was overwhelmed with the hundreds of smells. Humans, food, other animals. His nose amplified each lurching scent. Scents blew in the wind. Others were in the disturbed soil. Many of the scents were weeks and even months old, but some were fresh.

Near the water, Nate opened the plastic bag that Mike had given him and held it up to Boo's nose. Boo took a deep smell, filling his nose with the tiny skin rafts on the gauze. Dogs are the descendants of wolves, and with their giant noses attached to their active brains, they follow a scent to the source. Dogs follow scent in a track. Others follow it in the wind. Boo uses both his tracking and area scent training to solve problems. He stuck his nose in the bag and walked to the water's edge. Nate could not tell for sure, but it looked like ten or even twenty people had walked over the footprints of the missing boy on the beach. Boo placed his nose on the footprint closest to the water, the one where Caleb launched.

"It's too late for these clues to be preserved," Nate thought to himself. Still, Boo placed his nose right on the sand and affirmed the scent. Then he splashed into the water, nose up, moving back and forth. "It was a good start," thought Nate.

The good start did not last long. Boo came back to the sand, then back to the water a half dozen times. He was a golden retriever, a real water dog, and the moving water did not bother him. He ran down the near shoreline, but Nate saw frustration on his face. Then he crossed the river downstream and in the dark on the other side of the river, Nate could see his tail go up as he headed upstream.

"No!" Nate called. Boo turned and looked at his handler. They want us to search downstream. He called "Boo, come." Boo came along Nate's left knee. "Check it out," and he pointed downstream. Reluctantly, Boo moved downstream, working both sides of the river and wading across. The further downstream they went, and the closer they got to the other searchers, the less interested Boo became.

"After five hours of covering the river, Nate and his dog headed home."My dog is spent. He's out of gas," Nate told the command center on the radio. By then, other dog teams had arrived, and other searchers began coming in from neighboring counties. The sunbaked, dusty parking lot was full of cars now. Mostly volunteers and law enforcement, but press too. The radio traffic was heavy, but no one was talking about anything important. Nate stopped at the Command Center on his way out and downloaded his GPS tracks on the main map. On the computer monitors on the walls, he could see the tracks of all the searchers, and the hundreds of solid lines along the river where everyone had searched. He downloaded a track log from his own GPS and could now see a new blue line that went right down the middle of the stream. His contribution to a problem that was yet to be solved.

Mike was sitting at a computer terminal at the command center debriefing exiting searchers. "We are going to have to go further downstream," he told the sheriff. "He's just not in that part of the river."

"Dog tired," is how they both felt. So tired it was hard to move. So frustrated that they wanted to move. Wanted to continue. Wanted to find the nine-year-old boy they were looking for. This is what they trained for, but they had not delivered. They were too tired to give any more, and so Nate took Boo and drove slowly back to Lincoln, where Boo climbed into his crate and Nate crawled into his bed. They would go back in the morning if the boy were still missing.

CHAPTER 13

Nate's body slept, but his mind raced on. The open case, the open mystery, took over his brain, and in the fog of fatigue and at the edge of sleep he thought of other possibilities. Nate knew Mike was moving the search further downstream. He knew detectives were interviewing everyone at the picnic, looking for clues but also looking for a crime. Nate also knew the next day a helicopter from the state and a couple hundred more volunteers would show up, and he knew that all those people, all those trampling feet and poignant smells, would make his work and Boo's work harder.

In one sleepless interval, he began replaying the events of the day. He asked himself, "Did he miss anything? When was Boo most engaged?"

The idea came when his body was asleep, and his brain was in a foggy bank. It made him sit up and say, "Oh, yeah." Marie also woke. She was used to his law enforcement sleep pattern, but she was not used to midnight epiphanies.

"What is it?" she said, knowing he had been restless all night.

"We are looking in the wrong place," he said.

Nate tossed Marie the covers. He heard her say, "There is a lunch for you in the fridge," as she turned and pulled the blanket over her legs. There was a clean shirt and socks on the chair by his bed. Marie always said, "I am not a 100 percent homemaker type, but when Nate is on a search, all I can do to help is to provide clean clothes and food." Nate said, "Thank you!" in a quiet voice, hoping not to wake her again.

In the backyard, Boo was excited to go, but the fatigue of the previous day was clear. He jumped into the back of the truck and curled up in a resting position on top of a bag of gear.

It was 4:20 AM when Boo and Nate pulled out of the driveway. There was no radio traffic in the first few minutes, so Nate called dispatch and reported he was en route to Rotary Park.

"Getting an early start," Sally said, confident that the sheriff was not listening. "Yes, Sally," he said. "I need to find Mike. Do you know where he is?"

"He's sleeping in one of the trailers near the command center in the park," Sally said. "After 36 hours without sleep, he was relieved of command about 8 PM last night."

"What else is going on?" Nate asked. That was an open-ended question he could only ask in the middle of the night. During the day, when others were listening.

"We've got about 150 volunteers and the state helicopter coming today. They are supposed to be gathering at 8 AM, just after the sheriff's press conference," she said.

"Things are pretty quiet at the command center," a voice piped in. Nate recognized the voice. It belonged to a retired deputy who volunteered when there were workforce shortages. It is hard to get police work out of your blood.

Nate said, "Find out which trailer Mike is sleeping in. Tell him to meet me at the command center in 15 minutes. Tell him it is important."

The retired deputy agreed, glad to have something to do other than just caretaking the radios in the mobile command center. When Nate arrived, Mike was standing in the parking lot. He squinted at the headlights as Nate's truck pulled into an open parking place. Nate could see that he had tooth paste splash around his mouth and his shirt was not tucked in.

"I don't have you scheduled to work today," Mike said. "Your dog needs another day off to be ready…"

"He's fine." Nate said, wanting to cut to the chase.

"Look Mike, I missed an important clue yesterday," he said. Mike looked at him with a combination of doubt and fatigue. In the 36 hours he had managed the search, he had heard all kinds of ideas from searchers, psychics, and well-meaning family members. Now his most experienced dog handler was presenting another wild idea.

Nate launched his idea before the window closed. "Yesterday, Boo alerted on the footprints, even though they had been trampled. He worked in the starting area for five or ten minutes and eventually headed upstream on the other side. I called him back because I am thinking, you are thinking, we are all thinking downstream. He fell in, the current took him downstream. I realize the track is now 36 hours old, but I want to see if he crossed the river and then headed upstream. If so, then we are looking in the wrong place."

Mike was too tired for questions. "Ok, but you need someone to go with you and we are a couple of hours from having anyone to help. Besides, if you are right, we need to rethink our strategy. I'm not in charge anymore. The sheriff has about three layers of titles above me now. I'm sure he will want to…"

"I don't need anyone with me," Nate interrupted. "I do not want people contaminating the area, or helicopters distracting the dog," Nate said. "You keep everyone busy downstream. Don't change your plans. Tell the sheriff what I am doing when he wakes up, and after he has had his coffee. I think we can figure this out."

Nate turned on his headlight so he could see his way through the camp. There were people asleep in cars, in truck beds, in campers, in tents, and even on the grass in the park. Normally Boo would want to inventory the source of all these scents, but there were too many, and they headed down to the point last seen by the river. He took out the bag with the scent article. He let Boo smell it, then he gave the "search" command. Boo put his nose on the beach directly across the river. On the other side, he turned and looked at his master, encouraging him to come. Nate did not want to start the day with wet boots, so he picked out a pattern of rocks and jumped from rock to rock, arriving at the other side completely dry. As he stepped off the last rock and landed on the bank, his eye caught a disturbance in the soil. He took the headlamp off and shined it horizontally across the ground, then got on his knees. He placed the light on the ground eighteen inches from the disturbance, with the rays of the light cutting across the dirt, highlighting the slightly broken ground.

It was not his imagination. Nate took out his cell phone and checked the photo that Mike had taken the day before, and it matched. It was a dry footprint belonging to a nine-year-old boy who had jumped across the rocks to keep his feet dry.

Nate placed the headlamp back on his head and looked at Boo, who had already picked out a path. "Let's do this," he told his dog.

CHAPTER 14

Nate had been tracking with Boo for two hours before he could turn off his headlamp and rely on the growing sunlight. Boo had clearly established a direction, following a fence and a twin track into the foothills. Boo was moving fast, making it hard for Nate to keep up. In the track traps, the places where there was sand and soft dirt, Nate could see the 36-hour old footprints of a young boy, so he was confident Boo was not following a hiker or another searcher. When Boo seemed confused, or when the brush was dense and difficult, Nate went back to that old idea he had learned in training — "Trust your dog." Boo came through every time, taking detours, but always finding the track again.

If they hadn't been moving so fast, Nate would have looked for signs. Footprints or smashed grass. Boo's body language told Nate everything he wanted to know. His tail was high and wagging. Even though he was tired, he was excited. They came across a deer carcass or another distraction that would normally get the full attention of a dog. They would flush birds, and get warning calls from chipmunks, but they did not distract his working dog, who was fully concentrating on the problem. Both Boo and Nate were tired from the day before when they had spent the day in or near the water. There was new, untapped energy that came as they continued along the track. Hope can recharge the drained batteries of the human body and mind and cause them to burn bright again.

There was something puzzling. Nate was moving up higher into the hills, following the track of a boy who seemed to want to get lost. Searchers always try to find a door into the mind of the person they are looking for. What is he doing? Why? What will be his next move? This nine-year-old stranger to Wyoming seemed to be running away or running to something. Every time he crossed a fence line or a trail that would lead him to civilization, he went the other direction.

The double track turned to a single track. He crossed a meadow on the trail. The remaining trail dissolved in the meadow. On the other side of the meadow, with no trail now, Boo followed the tree line to a ridge, and Nate followed. Nate realized that over the ridge was a designated wilderness area. That was a whole new ball game. No more trails, more wildlife. A more difficult problem to solve.

Over the second ridge, Nate came to water, or more accurately, Boo came to water. He had been scenting it for a while. Engines need oil. Tracking dogs need water to keep their tracking nose working. A small, icy stream was just what the two searchers needed. Boo found a slightly soft spot in the sand, where the water would flow around him and cool him down. He was beat. Nate took a pack of hot dogs he had pulled from the freezer just before he left the house and fed four of them to the dog. Boo gulped each one in a single bite, then turned and sucked down another quart of water. Meanwhile, Nate dug into the only meal he would have that day, a brown bag lunch from Marie. There were two peanut butter and jelly sandwiches, which were not Nate's favorite, but they were high calorie and preserved for 24 hours without refrigeration. A turkey or tuna would be nasty after four hours in a hot pack. There were carrots and an apple, and three energy bars. He ate one sandwich, the carrots, and an energy bar, but he was nauseated from the lack of sleep and residual exhaustion. At the bottom of the brown bag there was a handwritten note on a napkin surrounded by a heart. Nate always saw the heart, but he did not always remember to thank her for the reminder that her love went with him.

After five minutes, Nate could feel himself wanting to sleep, so he got up quickly and pulled his hand-held radio off his chest pack, pressed the transmission button. "Command Post, 1J747," he called. There was nothing. He was out of range. The radio needed a line of sight to one of the relay antennas scattered around the valley. He hated the idea of climbing back up to the ridge to report in. All afternoon he had reported on wellness checks. "747, Central." "Go ahead central." "Code 4 check." "Yeah, code 4." The sheriff must have been listening for command to be so formal. No one from the command center had asked if he was finding anything. They were busy with their own version of the problem, and Nate was grateful. He knew that more searchers do not always make for a better search, but he also knew that the sheriff was under pressure to use all available resources.

Still, nothing brought attention like a missing or injured search victim, especially a kid. Nate knew that to avoid a helicopter fly over, he would need to make radio contact. Still sitting by the water, he could see a well-worn trail back toward the meadow. He followed it until he broke into a clearing where he could see signs of a camp. In the center of the camp was a large spruce tree, a great climbing tree. Nate took off his pack and his chest pack, stuffed his radio in his back pocket, and climbed towards the sky. He needed one more strain from his aching muscles, then he would settle in and rest for hours.

Ten feet up the tree, he called on his radio. Nothing. Boo was circling the tree like a wolf, whining and barking at his predicament. At twenty feet, Nate could hear radio traffic cracking, but he could not distinguish what they were saying. At thirty feet, he connected. "Central, 1J747 on a wellness check."

Sara jumped in. "Nate, it's been hours. Are you OK?"

"Code 4," he said. "Call Marie and tell her I am ok, and that I will be sleeping on the mountain tonight. Tell her thanks for the napkin," he said.

Sara came back in a clear voice. "I didn't get much of your transmission, except that you are Code 4 and taking a break." Sara had the benefit of a base radio with 250 watts of output. Nate's radio only put out five watts.

Nate started down the tree, glad he did not need to go higher. As he did, he could hear the sheriff's voice, but it was garbled. The sheriff was telling Nate that no one would sleep out tonight. Everyone was expected to be back at the base in the next 20 minutes.

As Nate dropped out of the tree, he saw something that looked out of place. The camp was just a worn patch of land near water frequented by elk hunters in the fall. For one- or two-weeks during hunting season, and for a week in the summer, this was home to an extended family of hunters and equestrians, or scouts and leaders who saw it as their own private wilderness retreat. You could see where tents were pitched, horses tied to trees, and over to the right, by another enormous tree, were broken bales of hay. Boo saw the hay too, and dove in, nose first. He thought he had made a find. Then Nate saw a non-natural something in the golden strands. He scrambled through the soft enclosure and found a three-inch piece of a package of Oreos. It was not faded or dirty. It was just hours old. This was the place where Caleb had spent his first night. His third night was coming fast. Nate knew that after 72 hours, most people were found dead. Not all. But most. Boo also felt the urgency. Talked to Boo in a low and comforting tone, something he only did when he was alone with his dog.

"Hey boy," He scratched his ears and Boo drank up the affection like he had gulped down water earlier. "Thanks for all your arduous work today. I know you are bushed. Let's take a four-hour break and then find this kid." Boo did not understand the meaning in the words, but he understood the meaning in the tone of voice. He put his paw in the air, like a high five, and Nate punched it.

Nate took an ultra-light sleeping bag out of his pack and stretched out in the hay. Boo jumped up on top of one of the intact bales, but then reconsidered, and crawled into the hay pile and slept alone beside Nate's leg. Before they fell asleep Nate set the alarm on his phone for midnight.

CHAPTER 15

The alarm in his stomach woke him before his cell phone alarm. He was not used to being this hungry. He fumbled for his headlamp in the pack, then opened Marie's lunch and unwrapped his second PB and J. No. He stopped. Caleb would need this. The energy bars too. In the pack's bottom were a couple of small packs of store-bought jerky and two dried out granola bars. This would be his breakfast. He washed them down with water purified at the stream last night. The iodine tablets gave the water a dirty look that he ignored, but the flavoring he could not ignore. The chemical taste reminded him of the days spent in these hills as a youth, when the streams were less polluted and clean enough to drink from directly.

No time for nostalgia. Nate stuffed his sleeping bag back into his pack, without putting it in the stuff bag. He quickly put on his boots. Nate was already dressed, but had added a jacket to his clothing layers. He called Boo into the halo of light from his headlamp. Boo sat at his feet, and Nate produced two of the remaining four hot dogs. They had been thawed out for over 12 hours. In his pack at room temperature. Dangerous for a human. Just fine for a dog. "You're going to need this now," he said. "You'll get the rest when you find Caleb." Boo took the gift in two bites, then turned his attention to Nate, waiting for the command.

"Search," Nate said in a bold voice, and pointed towards the hills.

Boo bolted left, placing his nose in the straw. Caleb had also slept there two nights ago, and Boo needed to remind himself of Caleb's scent. Then he began circling the camp, trying to pick up the track. It was hard because the track was over two days old. In minutes, they were back at the stream. Boo took his fill of water, and Nate filled his bottles, reluctantly placing water purification tablets on the top to kill the nasty bugs that could grow in him, but not the dog.

Then Boo crossed the stream without worry of getting wet, while Nate found a log and a rock. Boo had direction. He was tracking, but it was dark, and Nate had difficulty keeping up. Nate was also having difficulty staying on the trail, Boo came back, found him, and redirected him. His sense of direction told him they were headed deeper into the wilderness, a pattern he had expected since Caleb was deliberately running away. His lungs told him they were going up, so once he had risen a hundred feet, he pulled the radio off his chest pack and called in to the command center.

"Nate? Is that you?"

He recognized the voice of Deputy Mike Rich. The casual tone told Mike that the Sheriff was asleep somewhere. The signal was clearer than it had been since yesterday.

"Yeah, Mike. I'm up and searching again."

"The sheriff is hot as a firecracker at you," Mike said. "We finished our strategy meeting for tomorrow and the sheriff said if he had to divert any resources to rescue you, there would be "heck to pay." Mike knew better than to use any profanity on the air, since these words were recorded and stored.

"What are you doing up so late?" Nate asked.

"Oh, we just went over today's search area with a fine-tooth comb, and we are planning what to do with tomorrow's search. We got almost five hundred people here. About two hundred volunteers from out of state. The sheriff says we need to keep them busy."

"Sounds tough," Nate responded. Mike seemed to want to talk and unload the stress from the day.

"Yeh. The media are all over this. They came up from Salt Lake and Denver. Even have a couple of national crews here, so the sheriff is worried. He wants to look like we know what we are doing, but we haven't found a thing. Not a thing. Have you?"

"Yes," said Nate. "Boo is on track."

"Where are you?" Nate said in an excited voice. Nate had been ready for this question, and he read off the GPS coordinates from the elk camp where he and Boo had rested. There was a one- or two-minute pause while Nate plotted the location on his mapping program. Then he was back on the radio.

"Nate, you are fifteen miles away in the mountains. You are two miles into the wilderness. No nine-year-old boy is going to travel that far!" he said.

"I know," said Nate. "But he has."

"You ought to head back. Then you can show us what you've got, and we can consider it. I can send an ATV to meet you in the foothills. We can talk about it."

"No, no," said Nate. "I got to play this out." He thought Mike would not understand the "trust your dog" maxim at this level. "I'll know for sure by sunrise. Just give me until then."

"Ok," said Mike. With doubt in his voice. "I'm going to tell the sheriff that you are Code 4 and headed down for the sake of your career."

Nate was not worried. He knew that if he came back empty-handed, the sheriff would bend his ear about following procedure and not searching alone, but he would be like the five hundred other searchers who were trying to find a missing boy and who had failed. The only difference is that he worked at the sheriff's department and would have to see the sheriff every day. It might hurt him when it came time for the next promotion, but he did not want a promotion. He enjoyed being a deputy, but he could use a raise in his salary. Things were always tight in the Garner home at the end of the month.

"Thanks," Nate said. "747 out." Then he turned off the radio to preserve its dwindling backup battery. He was worried about his cell phone too, which doubled as his GPS. Nate had turned it off yesterday at the stream when he noticed that he only had 20 percent charge remaining. He might need it to take an evidence photo and pinpoint the location for extraction. If he did not have GPS, he could not tell a helicopter where to land.

So up and into the night, he continued. His headlamp was strong, and it kept a bubble of light around him so that his eyes did not adjust to the dark and he could not see the full context of his location. Occasionally he glimpsed Boo nose down in the underbrush. Nate could hear large animals, perhaps elk, crashing through the trees out of sight on his left or right. He knew Boo was working hard, tracking, because the big critters did not trigger his curiosity. He just continued to work, driving them up the slope through brush and eventually to a ridge. Nate had also seen signs as he clawed up steep portions of his climb. Signs made by a small human. Scuff marks. Broken sticks and branches stripped at arms level where the boy had used them as handles to pull himself up the hill.

As Nate approached the ridge, he placed his headlamp beam on the terrain ahead. It would take him 20 minutes to go the last one hundred feet, partly because his lungs were burning, and partly because it was steep, with loose rock and few grips. Boo was already on the top of the ridge with his nose in the air. He was not tracking; he was air scenting now. Still looking for scent, but not in the grass or on the ground, in the wind. With his nose in the air and his neck stretched out, he almost danced as he followed the scent. Then Boo paused, looked at Nate, directly into his light, then vanished over the ridge. At that moment Nate knew he was close to a find, but he did not know if the boy would be dead or alive.

Nate struggled in the loose dirt and rock, two steps forward, one step down. Sometimes he feared falling and twisting his ankle. He wished he had been paired with another searcher who could help if something went wrong. With a big huff and a small step, finally he stood on the narrow flat of the ridge. He had not seen Boo for 20 minutes. He did not know which way to go. It was completely black, and Nate did not have a sense of how high he was, or what was below. He turned off his headlamp and waited for his eyes to adjust, slowly pivoting and listening for his dog. He felt a light wind in his face coming from the unexplored side of the ridge. That was where Boo was. He was working down wind, following the air scent now, not the track. Nate knew that if he called "Boo, come!" that Boo would drop what he was doing, and return to his master. His ability to come when called had been imprinted since he was 12 weeks old. It was automatic. Nate did not want to interrupt what Boo was doing. "Trust your dog," echoed in his head. "Let him keep working."

In his four years of training, Boo had distinguished himself with one characteristic. Most dogs can find what they are looking for. The recall, when a search dog finds what they are looking for and then returns to the handler, is very difficult for a dog to learn. No matter how enticing, when Boo found the subject in training or in real life, he turned around and returned to get Nate. For every good thing a dog can do, there are also bad things. Boo liked to jump up on people, and Nate had spent hours training him to not do that. One time he had jumped up on a toddler and knocked her to the ground thinking it was playtime, and licked her face. That brought an angry parent who said, "Call off your dog. Can't you see she's just a child?" The child was scared only after she saw her mother was mad. It was Marie who intervened and talked the woman out of filing a complaint with the sheriff.

Nate turned to Boo's instinct to jump on people to his advantage. He did not allow Boo to jump on him except in the extraordinary circumstances of having a find. In training and on actual missions, when Boo came back to him and jumped up and placed his paws on his chest, then Nate knew for certainty that he had found what he was looking for. It was a way of allowing unruly behavior to communicate good news.

On top of the ridge, Nate found a rock and sat down. He was too tired to be sore. His brain was hovering in neutral. He had turned the search over to Boo. In the dark of a ridge, somewhere in the wilderness, he completely depended on the dog. This search, this job, this career, the life of this boy, all depended on the dog. He saved the batteries of his light, knowing that Boo would recall using his nose and not his eyes. He pulled his jacket hood over his head, and in the blanket of darkness, he listened and waited.

It might have been 10 minutes, and it might have been an hour, but below him he heard movement in the brush below. He reached up and turned on his headlamp, but he could see nothing. I took five more minutes before Boo appeared in the halo of light. He was panting hard, and his golden fur was dusty and matted. His legs were caked in dark mud, and his eyes were hollow. Nate could see he was running out of energy.

"You got something?" Nate asked.

Boo paused, collected his energy, then placed his right paw and then his left paw on Nate's chest. Nate said, "Show me." Boo looked back at him, asking to be followed, then put his head down and bolted back into the dark.

CHAPTER 16

Boo was spent but also excited as he spun back to find the subject that he had been focusing on for 24 hours now. Nate followed the sound of his dog down through thick brush as far as he could, but it wasn't long before he lost him again in the dark. Their training had been in the light, where he could see what Boo was doing. Now he was moving forward in the dark, trusting that eventually his dog would bring him to Caleb. Nate was sure that Boo had made a sincere recall. There would be a refinement and then another recall for the deputy, dog, and boy to be in the same place.

Nate would grab the branches of the bushes with his leather gloved hands to slow himself on the steep slope. His excitement was taking over. Yes, he and Boo had found people before, but never after spending a full 24-hour tracking, now almost twenty miles. He was moving a little too fast down the slope when he tripped on a tree root and fell and skinned his knee. He popped right up and continued, paying no attention to the damage to his pants and the open but shallow wound. Then, as a sliver of gray began to show on the eastern horizon, once again he was in tall trees. Nate had taken the easiest way he could find down, and so he did not know if he had overshot Boo, or if Boo was out ahead. Again, he stopped, waited, and hoped his dog would find him. Even though he had been moving downhill, he was breathing hard, and his heart was beating at a high rate. When he stopped, he calmed himself, drank water, and listened.

This time, his senses were keen. He did not know the condition of the boy. For a moment, he wondered if all this time they had been tracking a hiker, hunter, or a homeless person. His mind went over the clues that he had seen, the footprints, the scuff marks, the Oreos. "Yes. We were on him," Nate tried to wash away doubt. "What will we do when we find him?" "What will we do if he is injured or worse?"

Nate was mentally reviewing the medical kit that he had in his pack and checking through his patient assessment procedures in his head. He looked up to see Boo right in front of him. He had not heard him approach. This time, Boo looked like he had more energy. He had found water and was walking with obvious confidence. Boo jumped up and placed both paws squarely on Nate's chest, leaving muddy prints on his shirt. It was a perfect find indication.

"Show me!" Nate commanded.

The sunlight was getting brighter. Nate could see more now, so he turned off his headlamp and let his eyes adjust. Boo headed down and left. He was zigzagging through the trees. Light from the sun was conquering the shadows, and Nate pulled the hood from his jacket off his head so he could hear. He still couldn't see where his feet were landing in the shadows and thick brush, and he did not want to trip again. Nate could see the overall terrain, and he could feel the forest waking up. He guessed it was 4:45 or 5 AM. Nate had a good internal clock.

Nate crossed a meadow, and the deep dry straw grass crunched under his feet. He paused. The morning birds were singing. A squirrel chirped a warning sound, and then the birds went silent. Nate could see where the grass had been pulled up in places. Small patches of dry meadow were missing. Then he heard a voice. No words. Just a voice. He climbed up a small hill with a crown of rocks and stood at the top. Below him and in front of him, he could see Boo's wagging tail sticking out from under a tree. As he got closer, he could see Oreos, a red plastic tarp, no tablecloth, a small backpack, and a pile of meadow grass. Boo turned and with almost full energy he ran the one hundred feet to his master and without hesitation placed paws on his chest again. Then he led Nate to the pile of grass. As they approached, the grass moved, a head poked out, and a dirty face looked right at Nate.

After an awkward silence, the boy said, "I like your dog."

CHAPTER 17

"He likes you." Nate said in a calm voice, almost nonchalant. Boo jumped unrestrained into the pile of grass and rolled over the boy, then ran back to Nate for praise. Then back to the boy. Nate could see the boy fall back, smile a weak smile, and play with the dog. Nate retrieved the two remaining hot dogs from his pack and fed them to his loyal canine.

He said, "You must be Caleb."

"I am," said the boy with confidence.

Finding the boy created three immediate tasks. First, he needed to medically assess the boy. His training took over like an autopilot and guided him through a list to make sure there were no injuries or hypothermia. Next, he needed to contact the Incident Command and tell him he had found the boy. Finally, he needed water, Boo needed water, and he was sure the boy needed water too.

The water came first. The boy drank freely from Nate's remaining water bottle, passing it back to Nate, who also drank just a little. Automatically, Nate produced the last two energy bars, and they each took one and ate them together. Then, in a communion of the searcher and the subject, rescuer and rescue, Nate took the remaining PB and J and broke it into two pieces. He took the small piece and gave the rest to the boy, who devoured it just as the dog had devoured the hot dogs he had produced for Boo. After that, he fished the apple out of his pack, cut it in half, and gave the larger half to the boy. To his surprise, the boy took the last two Oreo cookies out of the package and offered one to Nate. Nate took it, not wanting to appear ungrateful for this generous contribution to the meal.

"Are you ok?" Nate asked as they viciously consumed calories.

"I think so," said Caleb. This is my second night at this camp. The first night…"

"Oh, I slept in your first camp last night," said Nate. "In your straw palace." Nate saw Caleb smile. "I don't know why you left that place to come here. It was sweet. A nice bed. Water nearby."

"I was going home to Iowa," Caleb said sheepishly. "Kinda a dumb idea."

"Yeah, considering Iowa is that direction," Nate pointed east, "You have been mostly heading south. Eventually, you would have ended up in Mexico." Nate laughed, wanting to lighten the tension. He wanted the boy to know he was not in trouble.

"I figured that out last night," the boy said. "I felt pretty stupid and pretty lost."

"Well, you did a fine job staying alive," Nate said with sincerity. "Your mother would be proud. Heck, Nate checked his language, I'm proud and I don't even know you."

"Oh, my mother is in Iowa. She and my dad parked me here because I had run away before," said Caleb.

"So, you ran away again?" Nate laughed, wishing he had not been so honest. "Well, your mother is at the picnic ground. So is your dad." Nate thought this would comfort the boy, but he could see anxiety go way up as he talked about parents.

"I must be in major, go to jail, trouble," Caleb broke eye contact and looked at his feet. "My parents are going to kill me, then put me in time out for the rest of my life."

"Not if I can help it," said Nate. "We haven't had a murder in this county for seven years and I don't think now is a good time to start." Nate saw the boy smile again. "Besides, there are about 500 people looking for you right now and they will cheer for you big time when you get back." The boy smiled again.

"Look," said Nate, "I need to hike up to the ridge again where we might get a radio signal out and tell them I found you and that you are OK. Then all those people who are looking for you can dry off and find something else to do. They think you drowned in the river. And we need to get a helicopter headed up here to pick you up. Are you up for a helicopter ride?"

"Sure," the boy said. This time, there was a big grin.

"First, I need to make sure that you really are ok." Nate went through an abbreviated list of questions he knew the medical staff would ask him on the radio. "Any cuts, bruises, or bumps?"

"No."

Nate checked for hypothermia, then let the boy drink the last of the water. He was always amazed at the quick effect of eating calories and drinking fluids.

All the time Boo had not left Caleb's side. Already like old friends, Boo was nudging him, and Caleb would return the affection with a hug or a scratch on the head.

"You stay here, and I'll be back in about 30 minutes," Nate said. "You will be able to see me the whole time. I'm just going up that ridge," he pointed. "The one you came down. And Boo will stay here with you." Nate produced a wool stocking cap from his pack. It had a Lincoln County Sheriff's Search and Rescue logo on it. Put this on to keep your body heat from escaping out your head. That food is turning to energy and this hat will help your whole body stay warm." Nate also pulled his sleeping bag out of his pack and threw it over Caleb. "You might need this too."

"As he turned and dragged himself up the hill, he saw the boy produce a stick and throw it from his sitting position in the straw." Delighted, Boo retrieved it and pranced back to Caleb. Nate did not need to give Boo the "stay" command. He was too busy celebrating his find with his new best friend.

As soon as he left the boy and the dog, Nate thought of the mother who was about to find out that the worst likely outcome did not happen. In his emotionally soft state, Nate thought of his own mother, then

Marie. He and Marie wanted children, but seven years of marriage had not produced them. It was a tip toe subject for her. It was always a tough conversation. She envied what mothers had. She hurt to the core when she saw a mother with a daughter, of a family van full of booster seats. They had tried to discuss "options." Adoption. Invasive medical procedures. It always ended in tears.

Still, that did not keep Marie from children and mothers. He assumed by now she was helping in the search camp, feeding the searchers, and comforting the family. She was so good at explaining what was going on in a search and how they would find the missing. She was the unofficial comforter for the sheriff and for deputies when they made death notifications, because her capacity for empathy went beyond anything Nate could understand.

Nate had never felt the void that Marie felt until this moment. This very moment. He turned around. From a distance, he could see Caleb and the dog in the new sunlight of the morning. He thought about how he liked the boy and wanted him to meet Marie. Nate admired his courage staying out now three nights without meals, shelter, or companionship. He liked how he talked to Nate directly. Not overconfident, but confident. He even liked his ill-founded plan to take matters into his own hands and walk back to Iowa. "If I had a son," he thought, "My boy would be like him."

The climb back up the ridge was harder than Nate had expected. Exhaustion had occurred hours ago. His tank was empty. His muscles were spent. He was thirsty and without water. Hungry and now without food. He had been on his feet for 26 or 27 hours, with a five-hour break that had offered no good sleep. There was no real urgency to call the command center, except that there were five hundred people scheduled to search that morning, and there was a devastated family clinging to hope.

At the ridge, he got a clear, unobstructed signal and called in.

"CP, this is 1J747."

An unknown voice answered. "1J747, this is CP, the sheriff wants…"

"Break, Break, Break," Nate said. Interrupting the dispatcher. He did not have the time or energy to listen to complaints coming from the sheriff.

"I've found a green bandana. Repeat. I have found a green bandana." Green bandana is a thinly veiled radio code for a subject in good condition. Law enforcement thinks that codes like this keep media and others who listen to police scanners from understanding what is really going on.

There was a long pause. "Please repeat." The unknown voice said.

"I've found a green bandana." So, the person on the other end of the radio understood, he said, "Condition Alpha. Now please stand by to copy GPS coordinates." He took out his cell phone, went to the navigation app, and with just minutes of power left in the device, Nate held on to his professional voice and read the GPS coordinates to the dispatcher.

CHAPTER 18

It was 5:57 AM in the command center when Nate's call came in. The radio dispatcher was the only one fully awake in the travel trailer that had been refurbished into a mobile command center. Mike had been in the dusty parking lot of the picnic groups for three days. He had been first on the scene when Marge and the Preacher's wife screamed. He had called in and organized the search and had been the incident commander for 36 hours until the Sheriff took over. Now, on just hours of sleep, and living on caffeinated drinks, he was assigned to be the on duty overnight commander. He was asleep in his uniform on the couch in the back of the command center, behind a stack of empty pizza boxes that had fed searchers the night before. The picnic grounds had become a miniature city, with the command center in the middle and a helipad on the baseball field. Two helicopters sat motionless like sleeping birds, with their blades drooping. There was a tent neighborhood in the picnic area for the out-of-town searchers, but no one was stirring. They were exhausted after each having covered miles the day before. There was no longer a sense of urgency in this search. Unofficially, the search was now considered to be a recovery. There were a half dozen camp trailers and RVs parked randomly around the parking lot, but they were also quiet. The RV closest to the Mobile Command Center was the Sheriff's. He wanted to show he was in command, but right now he was still asleep, exhausted from the pressure and the politics of a large, highly visible search. Another trailer, which had been donated by someone in town, a big, nice go-to-Arizona-in-the-winter trailer, was at the far end of the parking lot, away from everyone. It had been provided for Caleb's parents and any other family members who wanted to stay and wait at the scene. Aunt Marge had visited the trailer, and brought baked goods from the church, but she stayed at home while Caleb's parents paced the small hall between the driver's seat and the bedroom. Nate's wife Marie had also visited and stayed. On the worst day of their lives, she had become a family friend and confidant. She was the informal liaison between the family and the sheriff.

The parents had driven in from Iowa on the first day, thinking that Caleb had just gotten in the wrong car or something. When they approached the picnic grounds, they saw the helicopter slowly flying patterns over the river, and they could see searchers in the water with poles probing under the banks, and they thought that someone had drowned. It was only when they drove into the parking lot and saw the command center and the volunteers that they realized they were all looking for Caleb. His mom sobbed uncontrollably. Marie was the first person to come to her side. Then came the deputy and the search coordinator, and the sheriff. The parents stood in the scorching sun and listened to explanations about search strategies and watched the comings and goings. It was a blur. At first, they had found patches of hope in all the well-meaning activities, thinking that a cheerful outlook would make a positive outcome. Then they grew tired as they relearned the hardest human lesson; words and attitude do not shape reality.

Furthest from the family trailer, at the other end of the parking lot was the trailer for the media, but most had either booked rooms in the motel in town, or driven the 90 miles south to I-80 to find a "real hotel" that had a "real bed" because they had "worked so hard" and needed to spend the money in their travel expense account. In the first few days, this had been a big national news story. With time running in slow motion, hope had waned in the family, then in law enforcement and the searchers, and eventually, the media lost interest. Like a dying ember that found a leaky can of gasoline, things were about to change.

At this early hour of the morning of the third night of a dying story, reporters and crews from local stations were pulling up and setting up for their morning news. These were not "A" team anchors, or even the "B" team reporters. These were the "C" team early morning show place holders who were paid interns hoping for a big story break to show they have what it takes. They were about to get it.

The radio traffic from Nate had stirred Mike. It had been the first traffic for six hours on the special search and rescue frequency. He was fully conscious when he heard Nate say, "Condition Alpha." "Alpha means A." It means "all right." We had been expecting echo in the water. Looking for echo below the dam and falls. Ready for an "E." We got an "A."

Mike grabbed the microphone from the dispatcher. He wanted to hear it in plain English, not in police radio jargon.

"Nate, you got him?"

"Yep."

"Is he OK?

"Yep."

"Give me those GPS coordinates and we will get a bird up to you as soon as we can get the pilot out of bed and the helicopter fired up."

Mike copied the coordinates, and then there was a short official conversation about setting up a landing zone in the meadow and using smoke flares for the pilot. While they were talking, the dispatcher had plotted the coordinates on the computer terminal. Seventeen miles as the crow flies in the wilderness area. "That dog tracked for seventeen miles in 27 hours. Wow."

Mike looked back at where he had been sleeping just to ensure himself that he was not still lying in bed dreaming. He was smiling ear-to-ear, and the dragging fatigue of the last 48 hours had evaporated like hand sanitizer on a sweltering day, replaced by an adrenaline rush. The sheriff had given strict instructions that he should be the first to know if Caleb was found so that he could break the news carefully to the family. The sheriff, like everyone, was assuming the worst. Marie had worried that the well- meaning sheriff would spill the sad news like an awkward elephant. She hoped she would be close, ready to provide comfort for these parents about to have the worse day of their lives. In this quiet camp, where everyone went to sleep exhausted, no one thought they would wake up to good news. As Mike stepped out of the command trailer, he let out a whoop, using his long-lost voice from high school rodeo days. That was followed by a loud proclamation to the entire camp:

"We got him! He's OK!"

Then, just to make sure everyone heard, he found an even louder voice, and said it again.

"We go him." But as he finished that sentence, his voice cracked. He turned and saw the night dispatcher leaning out of the command trailer watching the camp wake up. Then Mike wiped the tears from his eyes.

The lights came on in the sheriff's trailer, and in 15 seconds he was out the door, stopping only to put on his khaki police pants over his budging pajamas. He stumbled into the dusty parking lot just in time to see the commotion begin. Caleb's parents heard the whoop, but not the follow up. They burst out the door of their trailer in time to see a reporter who had just made coffee for her crew throw the cups on the ground and run to find a camera person. Somewhere in the ball field, a dog began barking, and one by one tents began to glow as their exhausted occupants turned on their flashlights and lanterns to face the commotion.

A half dozen, now a dozen people were converging on the command center. Smiles everywhere. Without knowing the details, Caleb's parents stumbled with renewed energy towards the command center, only to see the half-dressed sheriff break out of the small crowd and half run towards them. The apology for breaking the promise of not telling them first would come later. Much later.

The sheriff's smile could not be contained. His professional demeanor was still sleeping in his trailer next to his gun, his badge, and his shirt. He embraced both parents with his enormous arms as they poured out tears of joy all over his matted pajama shirt.

"We got him," he said. "We got him." "He's up there," and he pointed towards the mountains that were silhouetted on the horizon. "Our dog… Our best dog found him."

A savvy television news camera person who was recording the impromptu parking lot celebration also took time to give Mike a high five. The camera operator had sat invisibly shooting video of the ups and the downs, mostly downs, of the last three days. Like most, he had been expecting the worst. The good news took his heart home as he thought of his own family.

But his moment of humanity had to be put on hold because the news team was getting ready to go "live" even though their audience was still in dreamland. They had turned on lights and were trying to coax the sheriff in his pajama shirt, even the parents, to do an interview. Both declined. The sheriff went back to his trailer and emerged with his shirt and his badge, then held an impromptu press conference between his trailer and the command center to feed the reporters the little information they knew.

"Nine-year-old Caleb Nielsen of Mud Pond, Iowa was found safe this morning at approximately 5:23 AM by one of our K-9 teams seventeen miles southeast of here, at the edge of Peace River Wilderness Area. A canine named "Boo" tracked him for over 24 hours from this location. We are told Caleb is in good condition, according to the deputy who is with him."

"I'd like to thank all the searchers…" He gave the obligatory credits that turned into blah blah blah. The reporters wanted more meat.

A young reporter, who looked like she was just out of high school, interrupted. "Sheriff, do you know when we might see Caleb?"

As she finished her question, the sound of a police siren could be heard coming up the road towards the picnic ground.

"That's the helicopter pilot right now," he said. "We're sending the bird to pick him up as soon as we can get airborne. Then we'll know more. Until then, I have no more information." He stepped away from the microphones and walked over to Mike and shook his hand and slapped him on the back. Then he looked around and shook hands with anyone within the reach of his arm. "Thank-you, Thank-you," he offered words of appreciation to anyone and everyone who was nearby. Then he turned to the reporters, who had turned the cameras off and said, "We would like you all to stay at your end of the parking lot until we can meet with Caleb, his parents, and the deputy involved. Please respect their privacy," he said, knowing each of these reporters was already thinking about how they could get an interview with Caleb or his parents before the "real" network reporters woke up in their beds at the Hampton Inn 90 minutes away.

The pilot ran from the police car to the larger of the two helicopters, took the rope ties off the blades, and began a preflight inspection. Mike had sent a paramedic with the pilot to check Caleb out, even though Nate had said he was OK. It meant that the helicopter would have to take two trips because four people and a dog would be too much weight, especially with a high altitude lift off. As the engines wound up, he grabbed four bottles of Gatorade and a bag of day-old donuts that had been sitting in the command center. He figured his friend Nate might be hungry and a little thirsty. Then he took a packet of uncooked hot dogs from the fridge in the command center left over from the night before and put them in a paper bag. He took a marker and wrote on the bag "for Boo." He handed them all to the paramedic and said, "Bring the boy and the dog on the first trip and leave the donuts with Nate."

CHAPTER 19

Before leaving the ridge to return to Caleb, Nate used the last seconds of power on the cell phone to call Marie.

"Nate?"

"Yeh, it's me. Are you OK?"

"Yes. I've been worried about you," she said, leaving a long pause for Nate to speak. She knew he might stumble for words, but he jumped in with urgency. "Look Honey, get out to the command center as quickly as you can. They are going to be bringing this boy, Caleb, in on the helicopter. I'm going to send Boo with him. It's a weight thing. Anyway, you'll need to take Boo after he gets out of the helicopter."

"You found him?" She was excited.

"Boo found him."

"Oh, oh," she said. Nate knew she was crying when his phone died. Even though the connection was broken, Nate ended the conversation by saying, "I love you, honey. Take care of the boy. You'll like him. His name is Caleb."

Nate put his phone in his pocket and followed his tracks back down the ridge, crossing the meadow that would soon be the helicopter landing zone, and into the trees where Caleb was camped with Boo. The sun was in full force now, wiping the morning dew from the tall grass leaves. As he approached the camp, he could see the boy was asleep in the sun on the pile of grass with his arm he had pulled from under the tree. His arm was around this big, blonde, beautiful golden retriever that looked like a stuffed rug lying next to him. It was a picture he did not take but never forgot.

Nate took a small smoke flare out of his pack that he had been carrying for years and never used. Then he walked to the meadow and stood, waiting for the sound of the helicopter. He watched the light breeze make exaggerated waves on the green and golden grass, and then in the recesses of heart and brain he conjured the nine-year-old Nate crossing the meadow, throwing a stick to his dog. He had come so far. He had found himself. He had found his vocation. He had found his Marie. And he had found his perfect dog, his work companion. Now he had found this boy. He had found this friend.

As he stood there in that moment, he felt a cool touch in his hand. He looked down to see Boo by his side, looking up. His deep dark eyes, his dangling tongue, his wagging tail, told Nate the dog knew what he had done. He knew it was important. Nate got down on his knees, and for the first time felt a bit of a pain in the scraped knee. He didn't care. He pulled Boo onto his chest and held him, scratching the back of his soft fur head. "Nice job superhero," Nate whispered in his ear with full faith that the dog could understand.

The sound of the helicopter echoed off the hills, and Nate pulled the cap off the flare and watched it burst to life. The tiny stick produced a steady column of orange smoke. He placed the flare on a rock where it would cause no grass fire. The smoke would give the pilot a sense of the wind direction at ground level, but the dimensions of the landing zone were obvious. Then he turned back to the camp. Boo was still exhausted, but with his limited energy, he arose and pranced like a reindeer around the pile of boy and grass. Then from a distance Nate could see the dog nudging the boy back to consciousness not for the sake of the helicopter and rescue, but to play stick. Caleb obliged and played with the dog until Nate arrived.

"Are you ready to go home?" Nate said over the growing noise. The helicopter swung over the ridge and contorted into position to land in the meadow. Then it made its slow-motion approach over the trees and into the open space above the meadow. As the pilot carefully lowered the craft the last few feet, defining noise from the rotors made the conversation difficult. Caleb nodded.

"When you get there, you'll see a sheriff, your parents, Aunt Marge, and reporters. You don't need to talk to anyone except your parents." Nate said. "You'll also meet Marie. She is my wife. I asked her to check in on you."

"What about Boo? And, what about you?" the boy asked.

"Boo is going with you. Are you OK with that?"

"Sure thing," said Caleb with excitement.

"You'll need to hold on to him, but I trust you with him," Nate said. He could already see a bond forming between the boy and the dog. Caleb felt it too. "Can I keep him?" he asked Nate. Then jumped in to clarify, "I mean not keep him, keep him, I mean be his friend. Play with him. See him again, you know?"

"I hope you will," said Nate.

Nate understood this boy. How he needed normal connection, trust, and he needed a friend. Boo could be that friend. He was not running away from Lincoln City, Aunt Marge, and Billy. He was trying to return to normal.

The helicopter had landed near the flare, and the engines were winding down, making conversation easier. The paramedic had jumped out of the left door and was gathering her gear, getting ready to walk over to examine the boy. Once the blades stopped, the pilot got out and handed Nate the bag of donuts and the Gatorade from Mike. Then said, "It might be an hour before I get back for you," he said. "I need to refuel." Then he tossed the hotdogs to Caleb. He said, "These are for the hero dog."

As the paramedic named Jill examined Caleb, he held on to Boo for comfort. Jill was a pediatric nurse who flew in the medical helicopter when needed. She had been the first on scene with a lost child more than once. While she was carefully examining Caleb for any injuries, and cleaning the scraps and cuts, she said, "Now that Boo found you, you are part of his pack. Dogs like Boo don't live very long. Just 12 or 13 years. So, they don't have time for friends. When they attach to someone, they attach deeply and stay attached for the rest of their lives." Boo listened carefully, his deep rich eyes glowing. So did Caleb.

Nate added, "I am part of the pack. When you get back to the picnic group, my wife Marie will be there to take care of Boo. She is also part of our pack. Introduce Boo to your parents. Show him off. I will be along in an hour or so. Ok?"

Nate took his leash out of his backpack and clipped it to Boo's vest. Then he handed the leash to Caleb and smiled. Caleb nodded, then took Jill's hand and stepped towards the helicopter. He took two steps, then turned around, paused, and jumped onto Nate with open arms. He held the hug for a long time.

In the meadow, the flare died, and the orange smoke dissipated. Jill stepped into the back seat of the helicopter and strapped in Caleb and the dog, using a harness and the leash. Then she gave Nate a thumbs up, climbed into the front seat, and the craft slowly wound up to full power and lifted 150 feet off the meadow. Then with altitude, the helicopter pilot placed the aircraft's nose down, letting the forward momentum and full throttle lift the aircraft up and out of the little canyon out over the ridge towards home. It would take less than 10 minutes to cover the country that Caleb, on his own, had covered in two days, and Nate and Boo had covered in 27 hours.

As soon as the helicopter passed over the ridge, the sound died quickly. With his donuts and energy drinks, Nate stood in the meadow until it was completely silent, and he could hear the birds again. Wading in the golden and green grass, he thought about how in the next minutes and hours Caleb would face his parents, his embarrassed and angry aunt, the throng of reporters, the questions of a Sheriff, with the puzzling emotions of a nine-year-old boy. Wow! That takes more courage to face the hoards than being out here in the wilderness alone, he thought. As he sat down on a log in the sun, and his thoughts wandered to his own family. It was just Marie. They wanted kids, but it had been seven years and there were still none. As his tired mind wandered, he wondered if there would ever be a little boy or a little girl in his life. Then his heart wandered to thoughts about that other little boy who was once been in the meadow. That little boy that was once him.

PART III: RESCUED

CHAPTER 20

Emily Smyth had come over to Caleb's house for lunch. After class, when he thanked her for sitting everyone in a circle, they exchanged numbers, texted, and even talked on the phone. Talked. Emily. A cool girl was spending time with him. She just lived two blocks away and went to church around the corner. In a momentary lapse of judgment, Caleb told himself she thinks "I'm interesting." It was nice that she seemed interested in his story, but he feared that once she had heard it all she would be back hanging with the cool crowd, and he would be in the rear-view mirror.

In his times of insecurity, Caleb told himself that he was so uncool that he did not even know who was cool. He knew Emily was cool, because he would see her talking with the other cool kids, who were cool because they were talking to Emily. Somehow, this logic did not get applied to Caleb's self-assessment. He did not think of himself as cool because he was talking to Emily. It was like he had a temporary hall pass to stand next to cool when he was with her, but then as soon as she left the hall pass was revoked and he went back to being just the "new kid."

Emily had cheerfully and confidently been introduced to Caleb's mom. Caleb told her, "We are trying to find a place to hang out on Saturday night and we were wondering if we could take over the downstairs family room."

Who is "we?" his mother asked.

"Oh, about six or seven of us," he looked at Emily and she approved. He had never been invited to a Saturday night gathering that included a movie, gossip, and video games.

"Sure," said his mom. "Sure," she was too agreeable. No tough questions. No "what are you all going to be doing downstairs?" She seemed overanxious because she was excited that Caleb was finally plugging into a social life in this community. To keep the teenage awkwardness at a minimum, she offered to fix them lunch. Before Caleb could object, Emily smiled and said, "Sure, Mrs. Ryrie." All the teenage awkwardness was coming from Caleb.

They ate turkey and cheese on sourdough on the front porch and made small talk. Caleb pretended to know about the football team and the changes in school start times, and the upcoming prom that Emily mentioned. She was really plugged in. As the food vanished, Emily asked about the second rescue.

"Caleb. You said Boo saved you twice."

"Yes," he said.

"But you only told us in class about being lost in the wilderness."

"Well, the second time is also a long story."

"I'm up for that," said Emily.

"Ok," said Caleb. Surprised at her interest. He would have liked to have had time to rehearse the story. He was beginning to feel safe with her and thought her interest was honest.

He spoke.

When I landed in the helicopter, the television guys all got pictures of me with Boo, and my mother running to hug me, and the sheriff trying to keep her away in the safety zone. I also had to keep Boo from going near the blades. Anyway, it made for a good video and for a while we were famous. NBC flew me and my parents and Boo and even Marie to New York on a private jet just to be on the morning tv show. We were also interviewed by all the other news networks. But within a week, it was all gone. The newspapers, the television, they had all moved on to the next big story and Lincoln River was the same old place.

I stayed in the mobile home on the picnic grounds with Mom and Dad for days, then moved back to Billy's room and Aunt Marge. My parents had a room at the motel, but it was ratty, and I could tell they wanted to go back to Iowa. "Just a few more weeks in Wyoming," they told me.

So, I lived with Aunt Marge and Billy and slept on the cot. Most days, OK every day, I went over the Nate and Marie's and played with Boo. It was a small town, so even though they lived on the other side of town, it was just five blocks away. They really enjoyed having me around, but they also gave me chores and asked me to help train Boo.

It was a sticky popsicle day. So hot that by the time you got the popsicle out of the freezer in the store, paid for it, walked out, removed the wrapper, and began eating, you were in a race with the sun to see who got the treat. The sun would whittle down the popsicle, dripping an unnatural red or blue or green syrup on your hands. You would eat it as fast as you could, even so, no matter what, you ended up with sticky hands. This was a real problem for kids who did not have access to a dog. But a clever dog would solve that problem for you.

Boo was just such a dog, would sit in anticipation. Once the cold treat was consumed, he would approach for his part. He would start on the right hand, and then the left. His enormous pink tongue fully extended, he would scrub your hands for flavor. I think he just did it as a service if you had a popsicle, but if you bought an ice cream sandwich, it was to his benefit. He would lash his tongue in every corner and crevice of your hands. First one, then the other, then back to the one. Then he would turn to your face and hope to clean your cheeks and nose.

I loved it when he cleaned my hands, but I didn't like the face cleaning. So that is where I drew the line. Hands, OK. Not the face.

On this sweltering day in August, I got a "Biggy" ice cream sandwich, but the line at the last non-syndicated corner grocery store in America was three people long. Three people could mean ten minutes, because people talked, asked questions, then shared gossip about other people I did not know or did not care about. So, when the ice cream finally passed into my lips, it was soggy and already melting. Bits of the deep brown wafer and the white cold but melting cream stuck to my hands as I ran around the corner and up the block to Boo's house. Marie had asked me to come by and play with him.

It had been about a month since Boo had found me in the woods. Since that time, I had been a welcome guest in the Garner home. Marie Garner was the devoted wife of Nate. Boo was the entire rest of the family. There were no kids, and there was no explanation about why there were no kids.

Marie and Nate seemed to know that I was a reluctant guest in Billy's room and was tolerating my time with Marge. They saw me as half hero and half orphan. And Marie and her super deputy sheriff husband, Nate, were just the people to welcome an orphan into their home. In the first week, they had told me to stop ringing the doorbell, and now, after four weeks, I have full access to the fridge. They knew what everyone knew: that my parents were somewhere out in Iowa working out their problems. They were paying whatever little money they had left over at the end of the month to a marriage counselor or therapist. This was a community where people believed that most problems could be solved with hard work outside the home, hard work inside the home, ice cream, and a little religion.

Now about religion. Mom and Dad did not do religion. They seemed to think that they had outgrown the need for God, or Jesus. They always talked about religions that were far away, like Buddhism or Hinduism, with such reverence. Those people were enlightened, but the people in the local church were just creatures of habit, captured by tradition. I had to get their permission to go to church with Marge, and at first, I was reluctant. Then I liked it, even though I was shy when I got called upon to read a scripture or sing a song in Sunday School.

Marge and her family were the kind of church goers who arrived early, stayed late, and sat in the front row. Nate and Marie, on the other hand, arrived just in time, and only if Nate was not on duty. They always sat in the back in case he needed to make a quick exit. They were quiet, even reverent, but they were also sincere in a way that I found to be nice. They came to church to feed something, not to show off. I would usually arrive at church early with Marge. To the relief of Billy, who really wanted his mom's full attention, I would wait at the stairs leading into the chapel for Nate and Marie to come in just before the service started and sit by them. I enjoyed sitting by them. I like the fact that Nate would sometimes fall asleep during the service, and Marie would whisper to me, "Let him sleep. He was up all night helping a trucker on the highway." The sermon was about that Good Samaritan who also helped a guy who was having a tough time, and it meant something to me because Nate and Marie were sort of Samaritans to me.

When they asked me to come by and play with Boo when Nate had to spend a day away doing police training, I was thrilled. They usually paid enough to raise my purchasing power from popsicles to ice cream. But I would have done it for free. I love going to their house. Unlike Aunt Marge's, I liked how it was clean and organized. I like how they were kind to each other. I liked how they liked, OK, loved each other and missed each other when they were apart. And it kept me away from Billy, who had grown to tolerate me but still did not like me. When I say tolerate, I mean he let me sleep in "his" bedroom, but he did not like it when I hung out in "his" space. So, during the day, when I was not at the Garner's house playing with Boo, I was banished to the kitchen or the backyard. I was a guest in Billy's house, but at home at the Garner's.

So, on this ice cream day when I arrived at the door, I walked in without ringing the doorbell. It had taken Marie a couple of weeks of chiding to help me give up the doorbell habit. "Hey, we know you are coming and so just come in and announce yourself," she said. About the second or third time I walked in, Nate was just leaving and Marie was, well, kissing him like they do in the movies. It was awkward, but it also hurts a bit. It reminded me about the times with my parents before they argued every time my dad went off to the library or my mom went off to one of those temporary jobs she would sometimes do.

Anyway, on this day, Marie was at the kitchen table with her laptop. She said that she was getting ready to be a substitute teacher the next day, and that Boo was driving her crazy. I usually played with him in the backyard, and when I had tired him out, I found myself in the hammock under the tree with him sleeping in the cool grass below me. It took an hour or two of the play to get to that point. "Why don't you take him over to the river and up to the swimming hole?" Marie suggested. "It's hot and I need some peace and quiet to relearn junior high math."

"Sure," I said nonchalantly. Inside, I was singing a loud song. The river and the swimming hole were the sacred space of kids in a small town. Grown-ups did not venture there unless someone was missing for dinner or hiding from punishment. There was a maze of trails in the willows leading through splash pools up to a dammed up deep pool with the classic rope swing that, done just right, would deposit you in the deepest part of the pool. Of course, rookies and people who could not swim well would sometimes let go too soon. Any kind of an injury would lead to a posse of parents cutting the swing down. Within days, a new swing would magically appear. This was a part of the kid kingdom. Parents could invade. The kids were in control.

"Make sure you keep him on a leash while you are in town," she reminded me. That was not to keep him under control. Boo was perfect at coming when I called. Sitting when I commanded. And staying, even though other dogs were calling and distracting. Nate, as a sheriff's deputy, needed everyone to see him obeying the leash law, even though no one did. Most dogs still ran free in the streets in this town.

I clipped on the leash, and to my surprise, Marie handed me a paper sack with a sandwich and an apple. "Keep him out until 2 PM," she asked. That gave me four hours of fun.

CHAPTER 21

Wow. Four hours. Four hours of fun in kid heaven with food and a dog. I expected that all these kids who had been eyeing me in church and around town would now see me with the coolest canine on the planet. A hero dog. They would see how this dog that everyone knew and everyone loved was my responsibility. Then, of course, they would want to be my friend. The thick wall of "out of towner" would come tumbling down, and I would no longer be "that kid who is just here for the summer," or "that kid from Iowa whose parents…" or "that kid who got lost."

I gave Boo the heal command. Then we headed out the back gate and turned right down the alley. At the empty street we headed down towards the center of town, but before we got to the only traffic light in town, we turned left and went three short blocks to where the pavement stopped, and the willows began. When Boo was asked to heal, he walked a step-in front of me, and with no tension on the leash, pranced like he was in a parade.

On this hot, sticky morning, no one was on the parade route. It was just us. At the willows, we followed what started as a wide trail that quickly lead across the stream at the far end of the city park. The park was empty, but trash cans had been pulled over. "Vandalism," I thought. I knew that Nate often caught young people in senseless destruction. "I'm never going to be a teenager who does things like that," I said to myself.

At the edge of the park, the maze began. Trails through the thick willow bushes, leading to water, leading to dead ends. Boo did not let me make a mistake. He had walked this trail before with Marie and Nate. I had walked it too. Marge had forced Billy to take me there with his friends once. They thought it would be funny to get me lost in the willow maze. I had a better sense of direction than they did. I had followed the sound of the running water, and watched the wet footprints, and gone right to the swimming hole. Billy was amazed. So were his friends. They were his friends, and had clearly been instructed by Billy, or their parents, or just the culture, to keep their distance from the kid who was from out of town.

On this day, there were no footprints to make the path. Still, I was confident that I would find my way. I let Boo off the leash and told him he was a "free dog," just like Nate had taught me. Boo quickly disappeared into the willows. I could hear him splashing in the water, running, then splashing again. It was dog heaven.

I walked for a quarter mile through the narrow canyon. There were places where kids had built forts, dug holes, and there were even single flip-flops washed down from the swimming hole. I went to an opening, and I knew I was close, but I could not hear the usual sounds of play. It was silent. Only the sounds of the water and the light breeze.

In the light wind, I smelled something. An unpleasant odor I did not know. My solo time in the woods had taught me to pay attention to those. I also had this image of the kids I wanted to connect with, the kids I wanted to know me, admiring me with the dog. So, I was disappointed when the sounds told me I would be the only one at the swimming hole.

To my surprise, Boo came up quietly behind me and sat next to me. His nose stretched into the wind. I had seen this before. He was not in play mode anymore. He was trying to figure something out. Just like I would scan the horizon with my eyes, he would scan with his nose. Back and forth, adjusting his body and his nose to catch the wind. Then he twitched and took a step forward, standing just in front of me.

His attention was focused on the willow clump to the left, between me and the swimming hole. We were standing in one of the few sunny spots, in a clearing of the pink sand and the river rock. There were no fresh footprints, but the heat and the anticipation made me crave the water.

I stepped forward around Boo. He stepped to his side, blocking my progress. Again, I tried to go around him, but his enormous body moved, to stay between me and the willows one hundred feet away. He stayed focused on the willows, now on both legs, then turned and pushed me backwards with his nose.

Just as I stepped backwards, I thought I heard something move in the willows. It could have been the wind, or a rabbit. Or a kid hiding, waiting to play a trick.

"Let's go swimming," I said to Boo, assuming that he could understand much more than people think dogs can understand. He turned and looked at me, all business, growled at the willow. The growl was not big or mean. It was not an invitation to fight growl. It was an "I'm here I'm ready to protect" growl. Then he turned and pushed me back again.

This time I got the message. I knew he knew something that I did not want to know. I turned and headed back into the willow maze. Back towards the park.

Boo walked behind me. His usual place was out front. He was behind me. Stopping to listen and smell. Halfway back to the park, he turned. He took five of six quick steps back up the trail, stopped and barked loud and hard. This time it was a mean bark coming from a nice dog, the nicest dog. When we broke through the willows and into the park, I could see the overturned trash cans and the torn-up garbage. This was not the work of teenagers looking for a prank. It was something big, something wild. Boo kept pushing me until we were on the city streets.

As soon as I got to the pavement of the city streets, Marie came driving up in the old pickup truck.

"Are you all right?" she asked, and I wondered if she was psychic. "Oh, I was so scared," she said in a dramatic voice. Marie was rarely dramatic. "Nate called, and I told him you were headed to the swimming hole with Boo, and he told me that there had been a bear sighting in the park and that the mayor and the sheriffs had closed it. I must be the only one in town not paying attention." Marie always made everything, including severe weather, her fault.

Just then, the police car pulled up, and Officer Phil got out.

"Looks like you found him OK," he said with a wink towards me.

Yes, it was the only police car in town, and he was the only officer in town. Nate was Officer Phil's back up unless he was issuing parking tickets or enforcing the controversial leash law.

"I called Phil when I knew Nate was two hours away. I didn't want to go into that thicket without protection," Marie said with a bit of apology in her voice.

"Did you see the bear?" Phil asked.

"No." I said. "But Boo did." I told her about what Boo did, how he kept me from. How he guarded my retreat. How he barked a warning bark. Then I told them both about the trash cans in the park and the garbage everywhere. Then Marie did something that I did not expect. Something for which I was hungry. Something that was rare in my family and that I had missed. She pulled me into herself and squeezed me. As she hugged without restraint, she said, "Oh Caleb. I am so sorry. I would have never forgiven myself if you had been hurt."

She held me for a few seconds, or a minute, or an hour. I don't know. Then she turned her affection to Boo with the same sincerity. Then pulled us together. I'm sure she was crying.

CHAPTER 22

From then on, things were different for me. My second rescue was not when Boo kept me from the bear, it was when I moved in with the Garners. Nate came home and heard the entire story that night. My version with just the facts, and Marie's version with all the emotion. When they took me home that night, I was sent to my room, or Billy's room, because "I must be tired and needed to get to sleep." I could hear the quiet voices down the hall talking for the next hour. Serious adult talk. Words like "home," and "overwhelmed" came wafting down the corridor, but I really did not know what they were talking about.

In the morning, I work up to the smell of bacon. Aunt Marge was making a big breakfast, and there was a pile of dirty dishes in the sink, showing that others had already eaten their "most important meal of the day" and had gone off to work. Aunt Marge had a different tone in her voice and an alley cat smile. The vitals were placed before me and before I could take the first bite, she said, "I spoke with your mother this morning."

My day was just beginning. Marge had already been up for three hours, cooked a meal for four others, done three loads of laundry, and spoken to my mother. I could tell by her voice that big news was coming, but I could not tell if it was going to be good news or bad news. But then I don't think Aunt Marge would know the difference.

"Your mom said that things are going well." Interpretation: Your mom and dad will not be getting a divorce (whatever that really is) just yet. Yet they still have work to do.

"They don't think they will be able to visit as planned for the Fourth of July." She zoomed right past that because the big news was still coming, even though I was very disappointed that I would not see them.

"And I spoke with Nate Garner last night," Aunt Marge said in a well-rehearsed tone. "We spoke for a long time. Your mother and I think it might be good if you go and live with Nate and Marie for the rest of the summer. They need help with their dog, and you could have your own room...blah blah blah."

News flash. My life is going from bad to good to great.

Marge was thinking I would be disappointed. She thought she was going to trigger abandonment issues yet again. No. I was elated. I just did not want to stand up and cheer and dance because I did not want her to feel bad at me, feeling so good. "Yes!" I said to myself.

There was a pause in the rational, adult voice Marge was using to try to convince me that there was some place better on the earth for me, some place better than her home, her house, her home cooking, her front from seats at the church, and her bratty last-born son who on a good day held me in contempt, and on a bad day made my life miserable.

Then another pause.

"Do you need to think about it for a few days, sweetheart?" she asked. The "sweetheart" was added to encourage me to put up a fight. It was all that I could do to hang onto the pause for a half second and then say, "That will be fine. When do I leave?"

Surprised, Aunt Marge said that Marie was coming by after lunch because I needed to pack up my things. So, I attempted to eat my bacon and eggs, then bounced down to Billy's room where he was still in pre-teenage death slumber. In five minutes, I packed everything I had in the duffle bag, folded up the old cot and stuck it in the closet, and loudly shut the door on the way out. Billy never moved a muscle.

Marie arrived 20 minutes early in the old pickup. Nate was on patrol somewhere in the county, and it was one of those days when Boo could go with him. So, it was just her and me. I got the impression she was as excited as I was because she kissed my forehead and thanked me for making myself available to care for their search dog. It was a little like the baker thanking the birthday boy for eating his birthday cake. As we walked out the front door, Aunt Marge came running up with the same hug she gave me when I had arrived, and a bag of day-old cookies. It was "sorry" this and "sorry" that, with assurances that I was not being banished, that I was welcome back anytime. Billy was standing at the end of the hall, and on his face, I could see he did not agree. I could also see something else. He had a touch of envy.

I lived with the Garners every summer for the next five years. My parents worked things out, but we still could not afford summer camp and things like that, so I got shipped off to Wyoming every summer. It was heaven. I had my own space. Outdoors, cool streams and fish, swings over the water, bears wandering into town, search and rescue, and a dog, a real dog who I loved and who loved me.

Caleb paused.

"I understand now," she said, taking the talking boy by the hand. Caleb could feel a special moment coming, and he didn't want to blow it.

"I can see why Boo is so important to you. He gave you Nate, and he gave you Marie."

Caleb just nodded. Then Emily kissed him on the cheek, and he turned bright red and felt like he was glowing, like light on the top of a little toy fire engine.

CHAPTER 23

Friday morning, I awoke early to the smell of breakfast being cooked. I showered, did my once weekly, but not needed, shave, dressed, and then grabbed the envelope I had penned the night before and stuffed it in my pocket. I thought about how much bad and good had happened in the week. How much had changed. How I had stepped across the line, moving from "out" to "in" at this high school that I never thought would embrace me.

At breakfast, my mother was surprised again to see me. My mother was in a strange mood. A cheerful mood. The kind of mood she got in when she was planning a surprise birthday party for my dad, because I never really had enough friends to fully staff a surprise party. Her face usually told all her secrets, but she was also tight lipped, so I had to guess what was going on. When I sat down at the table with still ten minutes to spare before I made the mad dash to school, she nonchalantly served me breakfast food, then asked if I would reserve the weekend for chores.

"What? The entire weekend?" I responded. "I've got homework and (awkward pause) friends… I want to see." It was a knee jerk reaction on my part. Too much anger in my voice. But once I digested her words, I realized that beneath her faux stern face she was smiling. Was this part of the conspiracy I could feel brewing?

My dad entered the kitchen, looked around, then immediately looked at his watch. He realized for the first time in family history I had beat him to the breakfast table. Not wanting to acknowledge the herd of elephants in the room, he changed the subject quickly.

"Mom tells me you have been hanging out with some friends lately?" my dad said awkwardly.

"Yup." I gave no more information, wanting him to think my social activity was routine.

"She says they are pretty good kids." He kept fishing.

"Yup." I said, sounding like I was trying to keep my personal life personal, but I also wanted him to keep asking just to see how much he cared. I also was proud of my social success and ready for a little parental recognition.

"Mom says…" Mom stepped in with a look that told him to be quiet. He was a college professor, and a good one, or so I heard. He was not the kind of dad who gave you his full attention while you spilled your guts. He was stuffy, stiff, awkward, and well meaning. If I hadn't seen it myself, I would have thought that he had never kissed my mom. Sometimes he tried to hug me, but he preserved his dignity and hugged like it was the first hug he had ever given.

"I was just trying to find out if he had asked someone to the prom," he addressed my mom defensively. Then realizing that he had said too much, explained, "I was reading the parents newsletter last night, and I thought you might want to…"

"Perhaps you could tell him about your high school prom experience," my mother interrupted with a sarcastic tone.

"Oh, you know you are the only girl I ever cared about," he said in an awkward but playful tone.

"Already taken care of." I held up the envelope containing the written invitation that I intended to give to Emily that morning as I rose from my seat, grabbed my backpack, and exited the kitchen and conversation.

"Gotta go."

I relished the shocked looks on my parents' faces, the dropped jaws, as I took my book pack from the counter and ran out the door. I knew they would pump me for details when I got home, but if things went as planned, I would not be home until late. If things went as planned, I would walk Emily home. She would thank me, then squeeze my hand and say, do you want to come in and plan our evening? I would blush and then say "yes." She would lead me into their living room, introduce me to her parents, and we would get that moment over with. I was sure in my prediction that Emily's mom already knew about the invitation. They were very close. Emily's mom got texts, honest texts, two or three times a day from her self-confident daughter.

I could have been dreaming. I had convinced myself that she had no other offers and would go with me. I had asked her friend, another girl, a friend, how to ask a girl to prom. "A letter in the locker," the girl said. Then the girl carries the envelope around to her classes inconspicuously, but everyone sees she has been asked.

"Has Emily been asked?" I said boldly.

"Not that I know of."

My intelligence completed, and the 24 hours of self-talk to social bravery, followed by the penning of the letter, I was ready. I walked casually up to her locker and slid the envelope into the vents on the locker door. None of the boys at nearby lockers even noticed, but three or four girls saw everything while pretending not to be looking. The secret was out.

Then a moment of horror. "What if I had the wrong locker?" One digit off and my life would be ruined. I fought back the dragon of fear as I slid into my seat in Mr. White's class.

I was five minutes early, and still the class was there and had been there for a while. They were looking at me and not looking at me. It was like I had something hanging from my nose and no one was willing to tell me. People were speaking in hushed tones. Did they already know about the big "ask?" They thought I had stepped too far out of my social position and asked a popular girl out. The spark plug in my brain was firing random thoughts that made my heart rattle.

Then she came into the room. Emily. Confident. Happy. Carrying a pile of books. She didn't look for me. No room sweep for her future dance partner. There was no small wave as she passed, or batting eyelashes as she looked. No. She went right to Mr. White in a serious business conversation. More spark plugs. More rattling.

I tried not to look, but I did. There was an envelope sticking out of the stack of books. Mine? I looked some more. Yes. Opened? Hard to tell. Oh, yes. Oh, no. This is bad. Terrible. She's going to let me down easy.

Then the cool guy came up to join the conversation with Mr. White. He handed Emily an envelope. It was a brown envelope, professional looking invitation, I assumed, into her waiting hands. A ten-page letter in rhyme that ended in an ask to the prom. Emily looked at it, then thanked the cool guy in a loud voice, touching him on the arm and gave him a smile.

I was dead. No random firing sparks. No heart beats. Empty. Dead. Humiliated. He had asked. She would go with him. I would need to face her kind but firm rejection. Then I would have to explain to my parents, who were as excited as I had been, why I would stay home. No, I did not want to go into a group. No, I did not want to be on the decorating committee.

As I was conjuring up ailments to keep me out of school until the prom was over in three weeks, Mr. White called the class to attention.

"We have had an interesting week. A week that I will never forget, and you might feel the same." He looked at me and said, "Thanks Caleb." "Now Emily has an announcement."

Oh no. I had heard, even seen, that in the classes taught by the "cool" teachers, girls would make a public acceptance of their prom invitation. Emily did not seem like the type, but she was taking the floor. She took the letter from the cool guy and walked to the front of the room. I held my knees together so their shaking would not be noticed. She turned and faced the room but addressed me.

"Caleb," she said. "You've given us a great week…"

"Where was this going?" I thought to myself.

"We have learned a lot about dogs, kind people, and a place in our country that we knew little about."

"What was going on? Good or Bad?" I am wondering. I managed a weak smile.

"Your friends," pointing around the room, "found out that there is a memorial service for Boo tomorrow at 6 PM on the hill by that picnic ground in Lincoln River, Wyoming. We thought you would want to go, so we got together and bought you a ticket."

She held out the brown envelope, and I stumbled to the front of the room with an uncontrollable smile.

"Prom? What prom?" I thought. I was going home where was going to get to see Nate and Marie. I was going to smell the sweet, clear Wyoming air and cry and remember with my friends.

For the second time in a week, hey, in years, I lost control again. I smiled. I laughed. There was even a tear or two. I walked around the room. People extended their hands for the "high five." I said thanks so many times I lost count. Mr. White cut in.

"You must be at the airport in 90 minutes. I've arranged for you to miss classes today and Monday, but your teachers say they are going to be extra hard on you Tuesday when you get back. Your mom is waiting outside to drive you to the airport."

Emily's outstretched arm turned into a big hug. The cool guy stood up and put his hand on my back. "Have a good trip, Cowboy," he said, like he was speaking for everyone.

Emily stuffed the plane ticket into my shirt pocket then said, "Now get out of here," she said, looking around the class at the smiling faces. "We don't want you to miss your plane." The class clapped. Hi fives everywhere. I turned towards the door. Somewhere between the hug and the door, I stopped, turned, and looked at Emily, the Cool Guy, and the class, and said, "Thanks, Really." I swallowed. "Thanks."

"Go get 'em, Cowboy," the cool guy said. The class erupted into applause. I turned, almost tripping over the now empty back row of chairs. Mr. White was standing at the back of the room, smiling from ear to ear. He extended his hand, and we shook hands like old friends. Then I stepped into the hall, not realizing Emily was two steps behind me. She said, "Hey Caleb! Yes, I will go to prom with you."

I turned and looked at her with a face that was later described to me as "really goofy."

CHAPTER 24

I was so focused on what had happened in class that I remember little about the trip to the airport. My mom wanted me to relive the moment, but I was looking ahead. So, she just chattered about different things in her past, including her prom experience. I do remember that my mother wanted to come in at the airport, but there was not time. I could see she did not trust me to find the right airline or the right gate. But I told her I could read, and I told her I knew all my numbers to fifty, and that I should be OK. Then I reminded her I had flown by myself to and from Wyoming for the last five years. She had packed a small bag and gave me six twenty-dollar bills I could spend any way I wanted. I thanked her, and she said, "You've got some pretty great friends."

"I know, Mom. And great parents, too." I shut the car door and headed into the crowd.

Once on the plane, I put on my headphones and half closed my eyes. I didn't need to talk. I didn't expect anyone to understand or believe. I drank when offered a beverage and eventually pretended to watch a movie. Mostly, I just played the events of the morning over and over in my head.

Boo had saved me. Not once or twice. But three times. When I was lost in high school, wanting but not knowing how to connect with kids who might be my friends for the rest of my life, he saved me. His story, the image of his blond mane and bold stance captured the imagination of Emily, Mr. White, the cool guy, and others, who now would call me "Cowboy" not because I was an outsider, but out of affection.

In Denver, I transferred to a small commuter airline, and the 45-minute flight took me north, over the mountains where I had spent a lonely night while Boo searched for me. When I arrived in Rock Springs, I was told a sheriff's deputy from Lincoln County would be waiting for me as soon as I cleared security. They would take me on the long drive to the far corner of the state to this unusual service for a hero dog.

That's why I was surprised to see the blinking lights of a Lincoln County Sheriff's patrol car on the tarmac as the small commuter plane pulled up to the terminal. As I came down the stairs, I could hear a familiar voice arguing with the airport security staff. "I need to pick him up on before he gets in the building. He's dangerous," the deputy said is a faux serious voice. Then the airport security person said in a sarcastic voice, "I think that's your prisoner." I ran towards the large deputy and caught him in a big hug just as he spun around. It was Iawani Kanaapu, a deputy who had been on several adventures with Boo and I. He was a Hawaii to Wyoming transplant who was always happy, even when he was being dressed down by the sheriff or yelled at by a speeder caught in the act. Of course, when he was a newcomer, Nate and Marie had taken him in. But eventually the community warmed up to his happy.

It was a strange scene as the hand full of passengers passed a deputy almost three times the size of me hugging his "prisoner" like I was his long-lost son.

"You the kid who helped train the dog?" the airport security officer asked in a gruff voice that was standard issue for law enforcement. I think he was trying to tell the deplaning passengers what was going on without making an announcement.

"Yes," I said, not feeling terribly conversational. We walked to the car and Deputy Kanaapu took my bag and threw it in the back seat, then motioned me into the front seat of the car. The front seat was not an easy place to sit because I was crowded by the radios and dash mounted laptop computer that swiveled over to the driver's side.

"It's better than riding in the back," he said as a form of apology. "If you ride in the back, everyone will think you really are a prisoner." He motioned with his head to the curious passengers who were cranking their heads, not sure if they were seeing a celebrity or a criminal. Then he quickly fired up the engine and drove through the gate in the chain-link fence where another airport security officer was waiting to let us out. He nodded as we passed through, probably grateful for the break in a routine that we had provided him in the airport that only got four flights a day.

After a few turns in an industrial neighborhood, he turned north on the main highway and headed towards Lincoln County. In a serious voice that I did not believe, Deputy Kanaapu looked at me and said, "The sheriff says I can't use my car for personal business, like driving civilians around, so I'm going to have to make you a deputy."

I was surprised. I thought he was joking, but he pulled the car over by the side of the road and flipped on the flashing lights, then he looked directly at me.

I twisted my head sideways, not understanding where he was going with this, but before I could open my mouth, he raised his right hand and looked directly at me and said, "Raise your right hand." I followed. He faced me as best he could with his seatbelt still on, and said, "On behalf of the Lincoln County Sheriff... Oh, what's your name again? I mean your last name?"

"Caleb. Caleb Ryrie."

"I appoint Caleb Ryrie as a special officer in the Lincoln County Search and Rescue Association, with all the rights and privileges, you know, blah blah," He pronounced the voice trying to swallow a smile. "I'm not very good at this kind of stuff. Put on your uniform."

He handed me a bag with a nice new bright red shirt with a sheriff's logo on the front and in big bold letters that said "Search and Rescue "on the back. It was too big, but I didn't care. It was cool. There was also a black baseball hat with the sheriff's logo on the front and "Search and Rescue" stitched across the back band. I was smiling from ear to ear. It was a welcome home gesture I had not expected.

I put it all on, and the deputy said, "Now you'll fit right in with the rest of the team."

For the next two hours, all the way to Lincoln River, to the picnic grounds, Deputy Kaanapu told me about how he, an island boy, had been transplanted into Wyoming.

Then he told me something that was personal for Nate and Marie. "After hanging out with you, they wanted kids. Year round, all the time kids. I mean, no one would be a better mother than Marie, and Nate, well, he would be an OK dad too. So, they adopted the cutest little guy. Came out of California. Just months old. Turns out he was an island boy too. They were so happy. They took him to the park, to church, everywhere. Spoiled him. And wouldn't you know it, six months later Marie announces she is pregnant. Now they have two kids, and they are happy."

I was eager to see Nate and Marie again and meet the kids. I assumed that Aunt Marge would show up with Billy, so I promised myself I would be polite.

CHAPTER 25

In a break in the conversation, I asked "How did Boo die?"

Caleb knew everyone would know the details that he did not. All he knew was what was in the newspapers. He also knew that his classmates who had paid for the ticket would want to hear more details from him when he returned.

Deputy Kaanapu paused and asked, "Are you ready for this? It's a sad one. I mean, losing that dog has been like losing a member of the family for the sheriff's department."

Caleb nodded affirmatively, but Deputy Kaanapu did not pause. He continued to speak in his soft voice that sounded like he was singing when he talked.

"You know, Boo was like a local celebrity dog. He would be with Nate whenever he was on duty, and sometimes Nate would leave him at the Sheriff's Office when he was on a call. The old sheriff didn't like that, but Mike is the new sheriff, and he loves it when that big, friendly dog hangs around and greets everybody. Kids would come by to see him. Nate took him to all the elementary schools. I think half the kids in Lincoln County knew his name."

Again, Caleb nodded. He remembered in the summers he had cared for Boo how scout groups and youth groups would request a "doggie demo." Nate was on duty and so Caleb, with the help of Marie, would take the dog to a classroom or a park, or sometimes a summer camp. He would tell a bit about how he got lost, then send a lucky volunteer out from the group to hide a hundred yards away. Boo knew the game, and would amp up his excitement, then as soon as Caleb took him off lead and gave him the search command, he would bolt like an arrow to the hiding place. Some kids would try to be clever and hide in a tree or lay out on the top of a jungle gym or get behind garbage dumpsters. It did not matter. You could not fool Boo's nose.

Within a minute, Boo would charge back. He would jump up on Caleb's chest, almost knocking him down, then turn around for the find. He would do that until Caleb, Boo, the hider, and the audience were all standing in the same place. Then Caleb would produce Boo's favorite toy and give Boo intensive play as a reward.

Marie would usually drive Caleb to these demo sessions, particularly in the beginning, but sometimes, when she was busy, and Nate was on a call, one of the other sheriff's deputies would be the chauffeur. As a result, Caleb got to know the deputies, and felt at home with law enforcement. He also became comfortable telling stories in front of a class.

Deputy Kaanapu continued. "We got a call to respond to one of the campgrounds by the lake that a five-year-old girl was missing. Where you and I looked for that autistic kid. It was already dark and getting cold. It was supposed to be in the low 40s at that altitude overnight. Nate brought Boo, but when we arrived, someone in the campground had already organized a search with volunteers, and about one hundred people were going shoulder-to-shoulder through and around the camp group. It's good that they cared enough to do something, but it's not good because now all the clues and track and scent that you might use to start a search are gone. Destroyed."

Caleb knew about search theory and canine search strategy because Nate had explained to him what had happened when he was lost. He showed Caleb once, when the river was low, where Caleb's footprints had been in the sand. "That is called the PLS," said Nate. "The point-last-see. The PLS is where the search is started. That is where you find the clues for the search. The problem with your search," he told Caleb,

"Was that we miss interpreted the clues. We thought you had gone into the water at that point when you went upstream. Boo figured it out."

Deputy Kaanapu was a superb storyteller, and it was clear he had already told this story to others. "This little girl was playing with her older brothers and sisters near the camp, somewhere on the south side. We couldn't tell. They started heading back to camp for dinner. So, they were halfway through the dinner when they realized she was missing. That's when they started looking around and asking questions. More people in the camp started looking. They were worried because the little girl just had a shirt and pants on. Not even a jacket. I mean you know what it's like in the fall around here," he looked at Caleb, and Caleb nodded, even though he had only been in the high country by the wilderness area in the summer. Even in the summer, he had seen frost on the meadows in the morning. It could get cold.

"To make matters worse," the deputy continued, "They were expecting a little rain that night." He paused for dramatic effect.

"So, everyone searched in a disorganized fashion for a couple of hours. About 10 PM, I got on the megaphone and called everyone in. We cleared out the area. And Nate started Boo at the PLS, where the little girl had been playing with her brothers and sisters. Boo was working slowly, because he's getting old, but his nose was still as sharp as a knife. Still, he was having a tough time, and after about an hour, he gave up. Boo wasn't going anywhere."

"By then, the search and rescue team had arrived and there were still volunteers who wanted to search. It was close to midnight, but Mike (the Sheriff) said given the 30 degrees drop in temperature, we'd better find the girl. So, they all went to the PLS, south of this campground. They assumed the girl would have walked south because no one in the campground had seen her. They paired up, and we all fanned out to the south. Nate took Boo back to the parking lot and started helping set up the command center.

"We don't know when it happened. At 1 PM, Nate missed Boo. At first, he thought he was sleeping somewhere, but he couldn't find him. We searched the camp and the parking lot, but no Boo. We looked for hours. I mean, we were still looking for the little girl, but they were also asking people to keep an eye out for Boo."

"The early morning came, and Nate came running in with his GPS tracker. He had forgotten that it was in his search pack. So he turned it on and found Boo's tracks from the previous day, including a track that led north, downhill, right along the road. Nate grabbed me and we followed the track down. Not far, two hundred yards from the command center to a drainage pipe that went under the road. Gravel and sand in the pipe were dry, and there was Boo and the little girl asleep in the sand."

How did he die? Caleb asked. He had seen Boo's loyalty to his subjects. It was called "pack drive" by dog handlers. When they told the dog to search, they were tying into an ancient drive to find lost members of the pack. So, the dogs were loyal to people they had not seen, had not met because they were on this never-ending quest to complete the pack. Fill up the family.

"We just don't know," said the deputy. The little girl said she had walked through the camp to the road. She could not figure out which campsite was hers. Then she thought she was at the wrong camp ground, so she started down the road. When it got dark, she hid in the "cave" so that she would be protected from the bears. She said she fell asleep and was very cold. During the night, she heard a nice doggy whimpering at the mouth of the cave. It came in and snuggled up to her, and they fell asleep.

There was a pause. Caleb knew what Boo had done, but the deputy needed to say it. It was part of his rehearsed story. "That dog went out on his own. When he could not search, he snuck out and found the girl. She was not far away, but she was in trouble. She might have frozen to death that night. But a dog's natural temperature is 102 degrees. They are warmer than humans. He kept her warm and kept her alive. He also paid the price. It was his time. He was exhausted, and cold, and ready to go."

"We got the little girl out. Of course, her parents and everyone were elated. The searchers cheered. Everyone was glad. She was in pretty good shape. Boo just lay there. He just lay there for a couple of hours. Nate held his head on his lap, and talked to him, but he didn't want to go any further. I just waited outside the culvert, in the sun, until it was over. Nate called up to me, go find a shovel."

"In minutes I came back with a shovel and Nate was standing there with Boo in his arms. Nate asked me to put the shovel under his arm, then he said, 'Wait here,' and he walked into the woods. It took about an hour, but he came back out of the trees with just the shovel, and he handed it to me and said, "Let's go home.""

CHAPTER 26

As we arrived in the parking lot of the picnic grounds, it seemed smaller than what I remembered. Smaller, but unchanged. The ball field that had been a helicopter landing zone during Caleb's big, but now almost forgotten rescue, needed mowing. There would be no serious baseball until the parks budget allowed them to cut the grass. There were a dozen cars in the parking lot, from Utah and Idaho. One from Colorado. Up on the small grassy hill, they were gathering. They had been waiting for me before getting started. In the crowd of mostly strangers, I recognized faces. The preacher, Aunt Marge, her daughter, Shellie, and her new husband, even Billie, were there. Supposedly, he had spent some time as an overnight guest of the Sheriff's Department on more than one occasion. But Marge said he was trying to go straight, and that's all that matters.

As I approached, Deputy Mike, who was the new sheriff, looked at me and nodded, then cleared his voice and turned to the group. "Thank you all for coming. From near and far, we came to honor this dog that has touched your life. Now this is not a funeral, or even a memorial service. This is a celebration because we are all part of the pack that this dog created. And we will continue to be part of the pack and watch out for each other for the rest of our lives." The small crowd nodded and affirmed.

I stood between Nate and Marie. Nate was bouncing a toddler on his knee, and Marie was keeping one eye on a little boy who was playing on the playground a hundred down the hill. She wanted to make sure he did not head towards the river. When she looked at me, she smiled a soft smile. I had grown to eye level with her now, and I could tell she was impressed.

Mike said, "Marie Gardner has a few words to say on behalf of Nate and the family before we eat. After her remarks, we're going to have a blessing on the meal that has been provided by members of the community."

Marie reached behind me and grabbed Nate's hand. She squeezed it hard, then put her hand on my shoulder and walked up to the top of the hill, then turned and faced the crowd.

"Thank you for coming. Some of you came a long way away. From Boston, she looked at me. From Salt Lake. She paused after each location, acknowledging the people she was referring to. From Denver, and Evanston, and Rock Springs, to pay tribute to this dog who saved your life or found someone important to you. Thank you. We were all touched by Boo. But no one more so than Nate. You all know Nate, she motioned towards him and he went into his "awe shucks" posture. They worked together for over ten years. Nate asked if I would read these words that he wrote:"

Superheroes do for us what we cannot do for ourselves. But Marvel got it wrong. Real superheroes weigh under one hundred pounds, have a wet nose, big hearts, four paws, and a tail. They cannot fly or smash through things. They work quietly, invisibly in service of us, even though their life expectancy is just 12 years. Their superpower? A nose that smells 300-500 times better than any human.

Boo the-Wonder-Dog is a superhero search dog from the Lincoln County Sheriff's Search and Rescue team. He began training at eight weeks old and trained every day of his life. He searched for missing people in Idaho, Nevada, Utah, and Wyoming. Some missions were over in minutes, others went on for days and weeks, even months. Boo loved his job, and he was very good at it. He had over twenty finds. Sometimes we were in the right place at the right time. But some of his finds were exceptional. Something only a superhero dog can do.

When he was just a year-and-a-half old, on a cold, rainy morning, Boo joined a small group of law enforcement officers to search a swampy industrial area for a man who had been missing for three weeks. The massive search area had been covered hundreds of times. Helicopters, ground grid searchers, drones, and specially trained cadaver dogs had searched the swamps between the train tracks and the freeway.

Before we began, Boo went around the group of officers and smelled each of them. This "scent inventory" helps him know what he is not looking for. Then we spread out and began working north, into the wind, around industrial buildings and into wetlands.

After about thirty minutes, Boo's demeanor changed. He explored pockets of scent in low spots and around bushes. I could see he was trying to figure out what it was and where it came from. Further north, we came into a canal, and Boo began licking the water, tasting the scent that was coming his direction. He moved across the wind direction in the scent cone, sometimes moving outside the search area. His nose was on the ground, then he would raise it up and stretch it into the wind.

After an hour and a half, we came into a dense swamp with bushes covering the mucky pools. Boo ignored the mire and moved back and forth with ever narrowing swings across the scent cone. Eventually, he settled into a dense collection of 10-foot-high swamp bushes. Without hesitation, he launched himself into the wet thicket. Thrashing through the vegetation, he quickly disappeared. I could see the tops of the bushes moving, then stop. He rested, then headed back to me. It took him two minutes to go fifteen feet, but when he emerged from the thicket, he jumped up and put his paws on my chest. (He can only jump on me when he has made a find.) Then he turned and led me into the swamp to the lost body of the missing neighbor, father, and grandfather.

What he did next, I will never forget. He shunned the praise and treats that normally come with a find. Instead, he went feet above the remains, cleared a place to sit down, and sat down in a guardian's stance.

I called on the radio, and eventually detectives and the medical examiners began arriving, and slowly Boo let go of his self-imposed guard duty. The three-week-old mystery of this missing man was over. Boo figured it out when no one else could. As we walked the mile and half back to the car, phone messages of thanks and congratulations began coming in. As if I had done something. It was all Boo.

That day we knew he was special. From then on, whenever I took Boo out, people would stop and ask, "Is that him? One family approached me in the parking lot. They asked, "Is this Boo?" The kids knelt and gave him affection. Surprised that they knew my dog's name, I said, "Yes." The father turned to the kids and said, "This is the superhero who brought one of our neighbors safely home."

Speaking in her own words now Marie said, "I loved that dog and what he did for us and our family. You all know that Boo died finding a missing little girl." Marie nodded towards a young girl and her parents sitting on the grass. "She was asleep in a cold place and Boo crawled in and kept her warm and alive. It was his last service. He was a superhero who did things for humans that we cannot do for ourselves. A hero's death while serving us is what I think he would have wanted." Marie's voice never cracked, and I wondered if Nate could have read this obituary without crying. She paused, smiled, and returned to her place next to Nate and next to me.

There was silence, and then, not knowing what to do, the people in the small gathering clapped a quiet reverent applause. At the base of the hill were six tables, and on the tables were the potluck dishes that everyone had contributed, including way too much potato salad, contributed by Aunt Marge and the Preacher's wife. As we headed for the food, Nate and Marie came over, and after hugs and small talk about how much I've grown, they introduced me to their children. Nate said the words I had been waiting to hear. "We're going to start a new dog soon and I hope you will stay with us for the summer and help train him."

"Oh yes," I said. "Where are you going to get the new puppy?" I asked. Marie said, well, Boo helped us with that," pointing towards a small minivan that was just pulling up. "He sired a litter four months ago." A man stepped out. He looked at Nate, who nodded, and said, "Ready for the puppy party?" I was puzzled.

Then Nate said, "Now help me pick out the next superhero."

Ten nine-week-old bundles of golden blond fur spilled out of the side door of the van and onto the grass. The golden retriever puppies instantly caught the attention of everyone, and like puppy zombies, every child dropped what they were doing and started walking towards the nearest one. Kids fell over and tumbled as puppies chased them, licked them, and nibbled at their ears. There was one puppy who was a little bigger than the others and was less playful and more serious. He smelled the tires of the car, the engine, the food tables, then he stopped and struck a pose. He put his nose into the wind and began to inventory the scents in the area.

The man in the minivan called, "Ben, come." And the little dog obediently ran to his side and received his reward of praise. After moments with the breeder, he broke away and came over to Nate, Marie, and Caleb. He smelled each of them in that order, then nudged Marie's legs with his nose. Caleb kneeled to pet him, and he rolled over on his back and exposed his belly.

"I think this is your next Boo," Marie whispered.

"Yup," said Nate.

THE SERIES CONTINUES…

The story continues with *Finding Asher: Book 2 of the Search and Rescue Dog Series* (publication date: November 2, 2023).

In finding Asher, Caleb and Boo are thrust into an urgent search for an autistic boy. When they find the boy, he does not want to come home, and dog, boy, and search subject go deeper into the wilderness to solve a mystery, and to develop a deeper understanding for people with special needs and others who are struggling with mental illness.

FINDING ASHER

CHAPTER 1

There was no music playing in Asher's head. No rhythm. No melody. Just blank wall silence. Then, from far away, the sounds of the outer world penetrated. First the background. The unseen bugs and birds addressing the sizzling summer day. Then a dry breeze overlay, rattling the brown leaves. Finally, the distant sound of water over rocks and the echo of his father's voice saying, "Go." Because he had no words for the sounds, to Asher they were just noise.

Asher looked directly down at the body, into the hollow eyes and the vacant expression. Clinically, he reached across his father's stilled chest and took the hiking pole out of his already icy hand. He slipped the strap off the wrist and pulled the pole into his arms and held it for a moment, like it was his father. Just an hour ago, his father had awkwardly held him, something he almost never did. His father knew spontaneous affection, like noise, confused Asher. But sometimes people in Asher's world had to touch him. Hold him. He did not know why.

Holding the pole, Asher began to reorient. He played the linear video tape of his memory back to find the familiar, to the car, the parking lot, to the rhythmic beat of the hike, one foot in front of the other. They were headed to a familiar destination. The trail, the lake, the camp, the overnight, and the visitor. It was the same routine to the same destination, leaving at the same time with the same provisions in the same place in his back. But on this day the rhythm had been interrupted. His father, his forever hiking companion, coughed, grabbed his chest, and then fell.

While his father clutched his chest and thrashed his legs, Asher had waited in the shade by a tree, casually waiting for his father to get over his ailment. He had seen such episodes when he had been parked in a care center when he was a boy. Asher looked over to see his father's outreached arms and his moving lips. He paused, but against his instincts, he moved closer. His father reached for him, touched him. Knowing there would be no reciprocity and hoping there would be no resistance, his father used his last strength, and awkwardly grabbed Asher around the shoulders and pulled himself to his ear. "Go," he stammered slowly.

Asher gave his father no comfort. He did not know how. He just stared with an expressionless face as his father went limp. His face relaxed. His eyes emptied. The music stopped.

Asher sat in the dust by the trail, trying to make sense of what had just happened. Lost in the cloud of surprise that would overwhelm a normal person, the only way out he could see was to find the familiar. Find the routine. Asher took the food bag out of his father's pack that had their familiar meals. White bread, creamy peanut butter, macaroni and cheese, spaghetti and tomato sauce with no vegetables, and energy bars. Then he picked up his father's hiking pole. Asher always had two hiking poles of his own. Now he would hold one in one hand, and two in the other, and he would "go." He collected his knees and ankles under his awkward but strong, tall body and rose. He stuffed the food bag in his pack, and pulled it on, right strap, left strap, chest strap, waste strap. It was over forty pounds, but for Asher who hiked every day with his father, it was not heavy. He was 225 lean pounds, with tree trunk legs on a timber jack body and a round, expressionless face. To most people, from a distance, he looked normal, until they got close enough to see his eyes. Or more accurately, see him turn away his eyes and avoid social connection.

From where he stood, Asher could see the valley below through the trees, and the peaks above him where the lake spread out in the gap between the two mountains. He looked at the hiking pole and repeated his father's last word. "Go." There was only one direction to go, towards the lake. He accelerated up the trail, hoping he could get to the campsite on the far side, where they could be away from other campers.

In less than a mile, Asher heard a noise coming towards him. Someone was whistling. In minutes he passed an overly friendly older couple headed down the trail. "Going to the lake?" the old man asked, too loud and too friendly for even normal people. His wife brought up the rear and paused. "The last part is pretty steep," she offered her advice. The pair were puzzled when Asher stopped in the same way his father would have, then stared at the trail and the forest and said nothing while the strangers talked. He knew if he made no eye contact and said nothing, he would not need to engage. After a few seconds, he put his head down and continued his rapid pace. He was to where he would stop just off the trail, at the waterfall, on the flat boulder, just below the spray. There he would take out the red bandana, and the plastic bag, and spread out the creamy peanut butter on white bread sandwiches his mother had carefully made to the expected specifications. One quarter cut sandwich in each corner, and a cup of vanilla pudding in the middle, with a transparent plastic spoon.

As he sat at the waterfall, the breeze blew tiny droplets of water in gusts over the eating boulder, but Asher was focused on the familiar meal in the familiar form. He started in the top right corner, and ate each quarter sandwich in order, clockwise. Then he pulled the top off the pudding container, licked the lid as a preview of the coming treat, then ate his favorite comfort food, licking the spoon clean and putting it in his pocket. "You will need that for later," he told himself because his father was not there to say it. After the meal, and back on the trail, the music returned to his head with each step. The comforting rhythm was the same, but something about the tune was different.

For only the third time in his brief career as a sheriff's deputy, Matt Kaanapu turned on the lights and siren. He pressed the gas pedal of the older, monster car sheriff's cruiser and felt the powerful engine push his 300-pound frame down into his seat. With the lights wig wagging overhead, the man who called himself an "Island boy," felt the importance of his job, though he was disappointed there was no one on the road to see his important urgency.

Matt had grown up on "The Big Island" of Hawaii, gone to college in Utah, and came to love the land locked mountains. His father worked for the Transportation Security Administration (TSA), security checking luggage day in and day out. So, when Matt was hired as a deputy in the Lincoln County Sheriff's Department in Wyoming to do real law enforcement, his family was impressed and poured out the respect for which he had longed. They did not know the big city departments had turned him down. "Too big," they said. "Out of shape," even though he had passed the three-mile police academy fitness run test by just seconds. He had been on the job for a year now, mostly working traffic and the local high school. Most days in Lincoln County were pretty laid back, like on the islands. But not this day.

Sally, the dispatcher, had called Matt on the radio, and warned him that the sheriff would call. In the back of his mind, he wondered if he had done something wrong, but as soon as the boss started talking, Matt knew differently.

"Deputy, we've got a problem down at the Silver Lake trailhead," the sheriff began.

"Sir?" Matt did not want to interrupt, but wanted his boss to know he was listening.

"An older couple from down in Colorado was coming down the trail when they found a body. They called as soon as they got into cell phone range. I huffed up the trail for a couple of miles with the paramedics and the coroner. We found this guy, uh," he paused, clearly looking for his notes. "We found 56-year-old Kevin McFarland of Colorado, clearly dead. Been dead for about two hours."

"So?" Matt wanted to connect what had happened on the trail with why the sheriff was calling him.

"So, it looked like natural causes. A heart attack or something. But we took our time because we didn't want a big shot Colorado attorney trying to claim that a bunch of backwoods peace officers from Wyoming did not know how to do their jobs."

"Yes," said Matt.

"Well, the paramedics and a couple of SAR volunteers brought him down in the Stokes Litter, while Sarah found his wife's number in Colorado. When I got in the parking lot, I called. Well, she wasn't in Colorado. She was three blocks away in the Lincoln River Lodge, waiting for her husband to report on. I went over and picked her up. My wife came along because she's good at these kinds of things and I was sure this woman would need a shoulder to cry on. We drove her over to the trailhead, hoping to have her identify the body, and as soon as she got out of the car, she cried, "Where is my son?"

The sheriff continued. "I thought she was just venting, but then she went hysterical. "Where's Asher?" Is he still up there?

Matt realized the sheriff was still processing this stunning revelation. His voice changed. He addressed to the new deputy. "Matt, we need Nate Garner and that super dog of his, uh." He paused."

"Boo," said Matt.

"Yea, Boo. To get up there and find this Asher kid before dark. He's a special needs kid. The problem is, Nate is in North Carolina at a search and rescue conference. His dog is here. Can you go over to his house and get that dog of his and see if you can get him to work for you?"

"Yea," Matt said, trying to mask the doubt in his voice. "I could try."

The sheriff did not hear the last part.

He said, "Get here as fast as you can. We need to move!"

Caleb and Boo lay in a pile almost unseeable in the uncut grass. They were as far from the house as they could get without leaving the yard. After playing hide and seek (Boo's favorite game), and stick (his other favorite game) to the point of temporary exhaustion, the two had piled into the only patch of shady grass they could find to escape the heat of the noon sun. First Caleb had gone down into the cool grass. With more energy than a twelve-year-old boy, Boo tried to reignite play for minutes by poking Caleb's exposed arms with his wet nose. Eventually the bold, handsome golden retriever succumbed, laying down with his nose in the small of Caleb's back, then placing his paw on the back of his neck.

If you looked at the two on this summer day in this backyard, in this small town of Lincoln, Wyoming, you would think that they were eternal friends. But that was not the case. Two years previous, Caleb had been dropped off in Lincoln by his parents to live with his Aunt Marge, who Caleb did not like. At a church picnic, Caleb had run away and for three days was the subject of a frantic search. Eventually, Boo found him, Sheriff's Deputy Nate Garner rescued him, and he was returned to the living situation he hated, with one difference.

Nate and his wife Marie had become his Caleb's friends, and their hero search dog had become his companion. Nate involved Caleb in Boo's daily training routine and eventually he and the dog formed a rock-solid bond.

That was two summers ago, and now, in the summers, while Caleb's father worked on his doctorate, he spent ten weeks in Lincoln Wyoming, sleeping at the home of Aunt Marge but living with Nate and Marie, who did not have any children of their own. The "no kids thing" was a topic that was off limits, but once after Caleb had walked home from church with her after Nate was called out on a sheriff's call, Marie told Caleb, "I hope if God ever blesses us with children that we have a son as kind as you are." As she said those unforgettable words, she tousled his hair, then pulled him to her in an awkward hug.

On this day, Nate had arrived early enough to get Boo out of his crate, where he slept at night. He opened a fresh bag of dry dog food that he found in the pantry and poured out the right portion into the bowl near the back door. Then he filled the other bowl with water. Boo always looked disappointed with his breakfast, but Nate insisted that he be fed only dog food and never people food.

After feeding and playing, Caleb noticed Marie was stirring in the kitchen. She had a late night, getting home after midnight because she had to drive Nate down to Salt Lake to catch his plane. He could see the unkept Marie in tee shirt and sweatpants smiling as she worked in the kitchen. There was a phone call, and Caleb could hear from a distance say in a smiling voice, "Oh, Hi Matt." Then her countenance changed from happy to all business.

Marie called from the back porch. She had business in her voice. "Caleb, bring Boo. There's a search mission," she said in a paced tone, with urgency but no panic. Boo was already bounding his way to the house. Caleb remembered Nate often said, "Boo seems to know when a call out is coming even before the people do." Then Caleb thought, "Without Nate, how is this thing going to work?"

On the back porch, Caleb could see Marie was making sandwiches and filling water bottles, just as she always did when Nate and Boo were about ready to go on a search mission. Caleb stepped reluctantly into the mudroom, muffling the spring-loaded screen door against his back as he entered the house. It was just enough sound to tell a busy Marie that he was there.

She began. "Matt called." Then she restarted in a slightly more professional tone. "Deputy Kaanapu called. He said there is a missing boy with autism on the Silver Lake Trail. His father died of a heart attack, and they think the boy might hide nearby. They want Nate and Boo, but Nate is gone. So, they asked Matt if he could bring Boo because he's been around when you train."

Caleb knew Matt did not know the first thing about running a search dog, but he had been a willing "victim" when Nate and Caleb had needed a second person for training.

Marie paused before she bagged the sandwiches and looked directly at Caleb. "Boo will work for you, if Matt stays with you, and keeps you safe, then you can give Boo the chance to find this boy." Caleb remembered how Marie supported Nate when he was called out in the middle of the night to find the missing. Nate would often say, "Every child is our child," and Marie would repeat it. "Every child is our child," she would say, with hope in her voice.

Caleb reached out and took the sandwich bag. Back in the mudroom, he took the hiking pack that Nate and Marie had given him for his birthday, the one with the "ten essentials for wilderness travel" and stuffed the sandwiches in the large compartment. Then he grabbed his jacket and strapped it on the outside of the back for easy access, in case there was one of the frequent afternoon thunderstorms. He laced on his hiking boots, then turned to ask Marie if she had talked to Aunt Marge. But before he could open his mouth, Marie said, "Marge is not answering her phone, and she is one of three people in the world who does not have a cell phone, so we are going to have to trust that this is ok. I'll call your parents if I must."

Caleb was about ready to sarcastically say, "Good luck with that," when he heard the siren of the patrol car in the distance. In what seemed seconds, the sheriff's cruiser rounded the corner, and the sound of the siren brought every neighbor to their window. He was sure that within minutes Marie would receive phone calls from small town residents, overwhelmed with curiosity.

Boo stood at attention at the front door as Caleb took the dog's search vest off the coat rack and snapped it on his back. The dog uniform that said "Search and Rescue" on both flanks told the canine that this was not a drill. Matt turned off the siren but left the lights on. He hopped out of the car and sprinted his bulky frame up the front steps to the porch of the old, white framed two-story house. As he approached the door, Marie opened, nodded, and Matt asked Caleb, "You ready to go?" Meanwhile, Boo scooted by the 300-pound deputy, ran down the pathway, and launched himself into the open back window of the squad car.

ABOUT THE AUTHOR

Scott C. Hammond writes about his experience finding lost people in the western wilderness with his dog Boo. He is a committed teacher (Utah State University), an award-winning author, a speaker, and is regularly heard on radio and podcasts nationally. He is also a member of one of the best search and rescue teams in the United States where he is involved with about 50 mountain rescue missions a year.

I love to hear from my readers, including the always amazing stories about your dog. Contact me at: findingscotthammond.com

NOTE FROM THE AUTHOR

Word-of-mouth is crucial for any author to succeed. If you enjoyed *Finding Caleb*, please leave a review online—anywhere you are able. Even if it's just a sentence or two. It would make all the difference and would be very much appreciated.

Thanks!
Scott C. Hammond

We hope you enjoyed reading this title from:

www.blackrosewriting.com

Subscribe to our mailing list – *The Rosevine* – and receive **FREE** books, daily deals, and stay current with news about upcoming releases and our hottest authors.
Scan the QR code below to sign up.

Already a subscriber? Please accept a sincere thank you for being a fan of Black Rose Writing authors.

View other Black Rose Writing titles at www.blackrosewriting.com/books and use promo code **PRINT** to receive a **20% discount** when purchasing.

CPSIA information can be obtained
at www.ICGtesting.com
Printed in the USA
BVHW040250290423
663235BV00002B/3